AS
MERRY
AS
HELL

ALSO BY JOHN CREASEY

The Man Who Was Not Himself
This Man did I Kill?

AS MERRY AS HELL

John Creasey

AS KYLE HUNT

STEIN AND DAY/*Publishers*/ New York

FIRST STEIN AND DAY PAPERBACK EDITION 1985

As Merry as Hell was first published in hardcover in the United States of
America by Stein and Day/*Publishers* in 1974.

STEIN AND DAY/*Publishers*
Scarborough House
Briarcliff Manor, N.Y. 10510
ISBN 0-8128-8128-1

Contents

1

Distant Laughter

POLICE CONSTABLE DIMITRY heard the distant sounds of music and of laughter, and as he looked across the wide expanse of dark but open land on the fringe of Epping Forest, he asked the quiet night in a tone of true bewilderment: "I wonder what they get up to over there." He stood beneath the light of a lamp, on a road which ran on through the heart of the forest, straining towards the sound. Now and again a yellow light appeared, and he felt sure that it was flame from a bonfire; felt as certain that the singers, the revellers, sitting around the camp fire, thrived on their shared merriment. Even when the flame faded there was a pale red glow, and often though he tried, he couldn't be sure

9

that the glow was not in his imagination; a form of wishful thinking.

How did they really live at Merryfield?

Was it a good idea, this community living?

Did they really share and share alike?

Could one walk out for a day or a week or a month and be sure one's children were looked after by others?

Into the quiet, drowning the distant sounds, not close by but seeming to come from a spot between him and Merryfield, there came a scream. It was wild and searing, like a streak of sound-lightning; a scream of terror. Coming so unexpectedly, ripping through the peace of the night, it went through Dimitry as sharply as a knife. He stood, rigid; heart beating wildly. He felt a quiver up and down his spine. But before a second scream came he threw off the momentary paralysis and began to move towards the sound.

There was a third: *Eek, eek, eek!* as if each was being cut off, and then released. The effect on him was not so great as before, but he shivered as he pulled his walkie-talkie transmitter from beneath his lapel. Years of training and two years of experience told him exactly what to do. Call Divisional Headquarters at Halling, a companion town to Epping, give one's position and planned movements, and make for the scene of the incident.

"*Eek!*" he heard. "*Ee-eek!*"

The scream was cut off, but he was sure he

could locate where it had been; felt convinced it was straight ahead. He began to move towards it, speaking in a controlled voice:

"P.C. Dimitry calling. . . I am at the corner of Rackam Street and Forest Road, proceeding in the direction of the Merryfield Community towards a person who has been screaming. . . The scream has been cut off abruptly. . . If the patrol car pulls into the left-hand side of Forest Road opposite Rackam Street and proceeds towards Merryfield Community they'll see my torch."

"Message understood," the man at Headquarters answered. "There is a patrol car in Wiker Street, it should be at Forest Road in three minutes. Over and out."

"Out," echoed Dimitry.

Now, he ran.

There was a wide path leading across this corner of the forest, a path trodden by thousands of picnickers and ramblers over the years. It led through small thickets and shrubs and across open patches of gorse and bracken-strewn grassland. If he kept to the path he could afford to run. He could see the red glow as he ran; a man in his early thirties in good condition, running didn't trouble him, but the possibility of tripping up did. A light flashed on his right, and made his heart pump. He saw the face of a youth in the glow of a cigarette-lighter, but the cry had come from much farther away than this.

"What—what's that noise?" a girl gasped.

"Pony or something," the youth answered.

Dimitry raced on. He saw other couples stirring among the trees, had no doubt they had been disturbed by the scream. Amazing how much one could see by night. A couple loomed in front of him and he had to swerve. He kicked against a tuft of grass and nearly fell, but recovered.

"What the hell—?" the man of this pair began.

"Police!" ejaculated Dimitry. "I need help." For the first time he pulled his whistle from his tunic pocket and blew. *Why hadn't he done that before?* The sound of the whistle could have scared off any attacker, might have saved a life. He blew again. Other couples, lovers, were moving away from him, only the man who had called "What the hell?" was following. From somewhere behind Dimitry a pale light showed; the headlights of a car.

A girl gasped: "Don't leave me! Don't leave me!"

No one replied, but a second man appeared from Dimitry's right and now all three were running. The second newcomer, touching Dimitry's arm, said in the clear voice of an educated Englishman:

"It came from the right, I think."

"Pucklebury Ring," the first newcomer declared.

"Sure?" gasped Dimitry.

"Sure as I can be."

Pucklebury Ring was a clearing in the forest which was widely used for picnics and children's games, touch-me and "he" and rounders and hoop-bowling and cricket with a soft ball. Dotted about the perimeter were wooden seats and some tables, even fireplaces; it could hold as many as five hundred people and not be over-crowded. In it were tall beeches and slender birches. The undulating light from the car which was heading towards the spot showed up the silvered bark of their trunks.

Another man emerged from a clump of bushes.

"Hear that scream?" demanded Dimitry.

"It was—it was over there." This man sounded scared, and he was doing up his fly, nervously. He turned to join the little group. For the first time Dimitry took out his torch and began to sweep the beam in wide half-circles. The police car was now less than a hundred yards behind and the headlamps would give them much more light. Dimitry, bitterly self-reproachful because he had not blown his whistle earlier, had a hope-less feeling that they would be too late. One of the men also began to swing a torch round, while the car's lights accentuated the shadows of trees in an eerie way; it was as if the trees were mov-ing, too.

Suddenly, he saw the girl.

She was on the ground, close to a picnic table. She had long hair which covered most of her face. Her legs were bare up to the waist, one knee bent beneath her. She lay very still. Dimitry checked the onward rush, but his torchbeam wobbled. The other's torch wavered about her legs, then about her face. Dimitry, controlling his movements well, reached her. Going down on one knee he placed the torch on the ground and brushed the hair off her face with studied gentleness. She was very young. Her lips were parted and slack, and he thought: no lipstick. He saw marks at her throat as he felt for her pulse. He could detect no movement and again he groaned to himself, if only he had blown his whistle and frightened the assailant off.

The others were close to him, their shadows dark.

"Straighten her legs," he said. "I'm going to try to bring her back."

He shifted his position so that he was just behind her. He placed his lips on hers and gave the requisite six quick breaths. He was aware of a man pulling down the short, dark skirt. He began to breathe into the girl's mouth, long and slow breaths now, all thought gone except the hope of resuscitating her. Breathing: *In—out. In—out. In—out.* The car had reached the fringe of the trees and men were running from it. *In—out. In—out.* Voices sounded. Men passed the spot. Torch-beams were shone downwards, on the grass, on the bare patches. Feet appeared within Dimitry's line of vision. *In—out.* From this position he could see the swell of the breasts beneath a square-necked blouse; milk-white skin and a gentle curve. Because she was on her back he could not see more. *In—out. In—out.*

She was breathing!

He could see the rise and fall of her bosom. *In—out.In—out.* Now his heart lifted with every breath he took in, even those he breathed out created a kind of euphoria and all self-reproach was gone. *In—out. In—out.* Another man appeared in uniform, kneeling. After studying the girl's face he said: "I'll take a turn," and, realising for the first time how near breathless he was, Dimitry backed away. The other man, Sergeant Bowles, bigger, heavier, not much older, took over, careful not to break the rhythm. Dimitry started to get up but was so dizzy that he swayed. He would have fallen but for one of the men who had joined him in the search. This man was short and fair-haired; the first one who had joined him. He steadied Dimitry, putting a hand beneath his arm.

"Ups-a-daisy!" he said.

"Thanks," grunted Dimitry.

"Pleasure," the other answered, and there was enough light to show his teeth as he smiled. "She's got a lot to thank you for."

"If she survives," Dimitry said, anxiously.

"She has survived," the other man replied. He backed away but kept looking at Dimitry who was breathing much move evenly and able to see

about him. Two uniformed men were among
the trees, obviously searching for clues to the
girl's assailant. So there had been three in the
police car. He saw more headlights approaching;
presumably they were those of another police
car. The other two men who had joined Dimitry
had disappeared, gone back to their girl-friends
no doubt, and away from the risk of being called
to give evidence. The fair-haired man went on:
"As a gallant lover I suppose I ought to go and
see whether my popsie has died of fright or
swooned from neglect or disappointment. It
took me half an hour to get her to this stage." He
bent down and picked up a pair of lace panties,
peach-coloured in the brightening light. "Souve-
nir. May I?"

"No," Dimitry said. "I'm afraid not."

"May I go back and get the reward of my
labours?"

"We'll have to ask the sergeant," Dimitry said.

There was something about the flippancy of
the fair-haired young man that he liked, but he
didn't give much thought to that. As the later car
drew up he saw that it was an ambulance. Now
the girl who had been attacked would get the
best treatment possible, there was nothing to
worry about. The sergeant stood up as the ambulance man approached. They stood looking
down at the girl.

"She'll do," the ambulance man declared.
"Can we take her?"

"I don't see why not," Sergeant Bowles agreed. "We can come to the hospital to talk to her." He stared down, and made, for him, a rare comment, for Bowles was a routine man, and phlegmatic. "Pretty kid."

"Asked for it, I suppose," the ambulance man remarked.

Dimitry felt a flush of annoyance which he did not try to analyse, but Bowles made no further comment. Another ambulance man came up, carrying a lightweight stretcher. They placed the girl on this with the matter-of-factness of long practice and began to carry her towards the ambulance. The wind fluttered her white blouse but hardly stirred the skirt which came half-way down her thighs. Attractive legs, Dimitry thought. Bowles bent down and picked up a small, yellow plastic sandal, and looked about, obviously for its pair.

"Looking for these?" called the fair-haired youth.

Bowles looked up, saw the panties, made a grimace which might have been intended for a smile and stretched out his large hand for them. The youth draped them over the big fingers with great care. Dimitry, almost mesmerised by these two for a reason he couldn't understand, nevertheless glanced down and saw the other sandal, half-buried in a clump of grass.

"Thanks," Bowles said, folding the panties. "What are you doing out here?"

'The original purpose was to prove my virile masculinity," stated the youth.

"Where's the girl you brought out?"

"I hope she's still waiting for me."

"Did you see anything that happened here?" Bowles asked.

"Not a single thing. I must have my eyes tested."

"I'll have you tested for something else if I have my way," Bowles said heavily, but with a touch of humour. "Sure you didn't see what happened?"

'Yes. I heard a scream and I might tell you that I resented it, the moment was one of rare delicacy. However, it was unmistakable and my popsie changed from a mood of writhing passion to absolute frigidity in less time than it takes me to say snap. Soon afterwards I heard what I thought was a herd of wild ponies but proved to be your officer. Never in the shades of Epping Forest have I known so many lovers spring apart in so brief a time. You know he saved her life, don't you?"

"Yes," Bowles stated.

"May I go?"

"I shall report that you were here and you'll probably have to make a statement."

"I will, gladly," replied the other. "I never did it."

"I wouldn't like to be sure what you did," said Bowles, and then he looked across the open land towards another car. He swung the sandal over the thumb of his left hand, in which he already held the panties. "You'd better wait a minute."

"My popsie will never come out with me again."

"She'll never know how lucky she is," retorted Bowles, with his gruff humour.

Dimitry was aware of this dialogue, which made him fairly certain that these two men knew each other. He was also aware of many other things. About them all there was an air of unreality: in fact there had been from the moment he had heard the girl scream. The first reaction, his belated use of the whistle, his run across the common-land, the finding of the girl, the kiss of life—my God, he *had* saved her!—the arrival of the police car, the fact that the unknown girl had gone off in the ambulance, all of these things were sharply etched on his mind, and yet there was a feeling that he could not have been involved in such events. There was another phase: the way in which the police had started searching: the way in which the cars were placed so that they carved crosses as well as tunnels of light through the trees of Pucklebury Ring. Now he saw two men coming from the last police car. One of them was Detective Inspector Scobie, the senior man on duty tonight. He was also the oldest. Dimitry knew him only as a man to whom he had occasionally to give messages, the same way in which he knew the Superintendent and

the Chief Inspectors, men who lived in a different police world from his own.

Scobie looked straight at the curly-haired
young man, and smiled; he had a long narrow
face which could look either droll or doleful.
Now, it was droll.

"Hallo, Clipper," he said. "What's your alibi
this time?"

"I don't think I have one," replied the man
called Clipper. "I'm relying on the good sense
and the compassionate understanding of the police to clear my name."

"Humph," grunted Scobie, looking at Bowles.

"He says he was with a girl, and he wants to go
back to her," said Bowles, flatly.

Scobie appeared to think deeply before he
spread his hands and said: "Well, why not? Have
a man go and help him to find her, and if she
really exists then we can use that good sense he's
relying on." He dismissed the man he called
Clipper with a nod, and turned to Dimitry. He
pursed his lips, gave another droll smile, and
went on: "Good to know you were so quick-
witted, Dimitry. I would like you to tell me exactly what happened from the first moment you
realised there was trouble." There was something so reassuring about his manner that
Dimitry felt completely at ease, but he hadn't
even opened his mouth when there was a shout
from one of the men searching the broken

ground of Pucklebury Ring. It was a single, high-pitched:

"Hey!"

It made everyone turn their heads, while Clipper and his escort, now some distance from Dimitry, spun around. The policeman who had shouted was just within range of the headlamp beams, one hand raised above his head, looking towards the ground. The man with him, perhaps twenty feet away, called:

"What is it?"

The answer came with crystal clarity yet there was a tremor in the policeman's voice.

"I've found a body!" he declared.

2

Identification

To CAROL SMITH, what had happened was a nightmare, hazy, frightening. The most awful sensation had been the pressure at her throat. His thumbs. She could feel the pressure now; recall the pain it had caused, the numbed, pins-and-needles feeling at the back of her mouth, in her nose, in her eyes and her forehead. She could remember screaming. She could remember the way he had clutched at her and how she had screamed. She could remember turning her head from side to side in terror and his thumbs and fingers slipping, sometimes freeing her windpipe enough for her to scream before he got a firm hold again.

She could remember blackness.

She could feel his weight on her.

She could feel him become actually part of her.

She could feel the sharpness of his fingers, afterwards, when he had changed from lover to killer.

But now, lying here, knowing she was in a private ward at the Sibley Hospital, that a nurse kept coming in and out, that doctors had examined her, that a policewoman sat in a corner, looking through a magazine, glancing at her every now and again, she tried to forget it.

She felt sleepy and dazed—but above all else, ashamed.

Whenever she thought of what she had done, of what she had allowed Lionel to do, she felt cold shivers of repugnance. Yet even so, despite all the nightmare recollections, the fear, the shame, she had a sense of wonder at what had happened, of the ecstasy of the few moments when he had been with her. It was like a far-off view of sunshine seen through the blackness of a storm. First glory; then pain; finally shame. It was as if he had been two men: first lover, then would-be killer.

Why had he changed?

She turned her head, restlessly. Her whole body seemed to be aquiver with nerves. She opened her eyes and saw the policewoman looking at her; the woman had very narrow features and a long nose, and beautiful brown eyes caught by a reflection of the sun in a glass of water on the table near the bed. Carol closed her own eyes and shut out that picture, but the one which replaced it was of the dark shape above her, of the pale blur of Lionel's face, of the glint in his eyes before she had lost herself in passion and then, suddenly, in the fear which had replaced it.

"Are you awake, Carol?" the policewoman asked.

She didn't answer.

"It would be better to let me know if you are."

Carol opened her eyes again and studied the woman through her lashes. She was smiling faintly, lips parted; her mouth was quite large but puckered. Puckered. *Pucklebury Ring*. Tears misted Carol's eyes and she could not see clearly. She heard a movement, the creak of a chair followed by a touch on her shoulder. When she could see clearly again, the policewoman was bending over her; she sat at the side of the bed without taking her hand off Carol's shoulder.

"I know it's a silly thing to say," she said, "but try not to worry so much."

"I feel—I feel so awful!" Carol muttered.

"Of course you do. But you will soon begin to feel better. You're alive, you know."

"I—I wish I weren't!" exploded Carol.

"You'd be surprised how many times I've heard that said by girls who've later become as happy and contented as young women can be.

Carol, things will improve enormously. Nothing from now on will be as bad as you expect it will. And if you can only make yourself believe that, if you can keep calm inside, you'll be surprised how quickly the worst will be over."

Carol thought: How *can* I keep calm?

And she thought: It's easy for her to talk.

And she thought: What will Daddy do? What *will* he do?

The tears welled up again. She thought the policewoman would go on talking, but instead she gave a little cough and sat silent. Her hand was growing warm on Carol's shoulder when at last she removed it. Carol, eyes closed, could 'see' her father; the grey eyes; the dark beard; the swept-back mane of hair. It was not only that she had brought shame on herself but on him.

It was as if she had betrayed him.

And it was as if she had hurt him beyond all measure and in doing so had brought unbearable pain upon herself.

"Carol," the policewoman said quietly, but firmly.

Why doesn't she leave me alone? Carol cried within herself. *Why doesn't she go away?* And then suddenly, like a flash of light in darkness, she thought with a sense of shock: *Carol.* How does she know my name? She opened her eyes wide. The woman was now looking out of a small window and her profile was towards Carol. It was finely etched, a rather masculine profile:

long nose and pointed chin, both had a bony appearance; and she was very thin. She had a honey-brown complexion and wore only a touch of lipstick.

"What is it?" the policewoman asked.

"How—how do you know my name?"

"You were recognised by one of our police officers," the other answered, and then went on: "So you didn't have a handbag with you?"

"No."

"Did you know your assailant?" asked the policewoman, and then went on as if in afterthought: "I'm Police Constable Bessington, known to everyone as Bess, of course!" She moved closer to the bed as if to get Carol into better perspective. "Did you know him, dear?"

Carol looked away from her, towards the window, almost glad that sunlight made everything difficult to see; the brightness of all the things in the room faded. Of course she knew Lionel. Did this woman think she would give herself to a stranger? Even go into the wood with one? She felt a stirring of indignation but it quickly faded into shame; she might as well have gone with a stranger as with a man who really belonged to someone else.

"Carol," Police Constable Bessington said, her voice suddenly firmer. "You don't have to talk to me but you will have to make a statement sooner or later. This way can be much less embarrassing, and there are things I can keep out of my

official report which would have to go in if the
interview were more formal. I would like to
help, if you'll let me."

Somehow, Carol found herself looking straight
at this Bess. And she felt herself warming to her.
Obviously it was a fact that she would have to talk
to someone, would have to tell everything, and
this was almost certainly the best way. She could
not prevent herself from saying:

"I feel—feel so ashamed."

"Would you have felt ashamed if things had
gone differently?" asked P.C. Bessington quietly.
"If you and your lover had gone straight back to
Merryfield unnoticed, would you have been
ashamed then?" She added in that afterthought
way she had before: 'He did come from the
Community, didn't he?"

"Yes," Carol replied.

"Was he a friend?"

"Yes, he—" Carol felt her throat go dry. "We
are all friends there."

"That sounds remarkable," the policewoman
remarked.

"It is remarkable," Carol declared. Again her
throat went dry. "We *are* all friends. That—that's
what Merryfield is about. And that's why I feel
so—so dreadful."

"You mean, you went with a friend of a friend
last night?"

"Yes," Carol answered in a voice which was
nearly inaudible.

"The husband of one of the women in the Community?" asked Bess.

"Ye-yes."

"Did she know?"

"Of course not!"

"I'm sorry if I seem absurd," responded Bess, "but some Communities rather like Merryfield believe in and practise free love, don't they? I know of one where communal property includes everyone as well as everything." There was a hint of laughter in her voice. "Isn't that true at Merryfield?"

"Good heavens, *no!*" breathed Carol. "It's absolutely the other way round. Marriage—marriage is considered of great importance. Inviolate." She closed her eyes to keep back tears, and it was some time before she went on, her voice hardly carrying across the room.

"Do you mean all the couples who live together at Merryfield are married?" The police-woman obviously cast doubt on such a claim, and moved to put a hand on Carol's arm. She had grown into a striking figure and now she seemed quite aggressive and challenging. "I've heard that the contrary is true."

"In a way it is," Carol admitted. "We consider people who live together to be married in spirit. We feel that if they've made vows to themselves, and surely they must have before living together as man and wife, then that is a bond enough. While they live together at Merryfield they have their own cottage or rooms, and have obligations to each other. Each works to help support the other and children. If they have children, the children are given the names of both parents and at the least suspicion of infidelity, my father points out how bad this is for the Community. He—"

Carol caught her breath.

Her father had hovered at the back of her mind ever since she had come round, but she had not pictured him so vividly before. Now, she saw not only his beard and his face but his flashing, burning eyes; and she could "hear" his powerful resonant voice, condemning the faithless. What had she done? Why had she allowed Lionel to go with her? She could feel his hand about her now, easing off the flimsy clothes she wore; roaming. And she could feel the passion for him rising, a magic in the touch of his fingers that drove out everything else but the drawing of all sensation into the centre of her body.

She whispered: "I must be a harlot to give myself to a man who belonged to someone else. I must be—"

"Stop that nonsense!" exclaimed Police Constable Bessington sharply. "Once you start feeling sorry for yourself you might as well give up. Carol, did you know the man well?'

"Yes," Carol answered.

"Who was he?"

The answer seemed to be forced out of her as

she said in a whisper: "Lionael—Lionel Wil—
Lionel Wilberforce."

"A married man?"

"In—in the eyes of the Community, yes."

"Married to a friend of yours?"

'Yes," Carol answered in a voice so hoarse it
seemed to hurt with every syllable. "Yes. Mary—
Mary Lee-Wilberforce." Oh, God, she thought,
what had she done? Could she have been in her
right senses? She fought back tears which
burned her eyes and burned her throat until she
could not speak at all. She lay on her back, remembering, hating herself; remembering the
shameful pleasure. Dear God, how could she
make amends? What had possessed her? That
was the truth, she had been possessed. . .by the
devil. What else could it have been? She had
loved Lionel almost since they had met three
years ago; there was some quality in him which
attracted her in such a way as she had never
known. His touch, by accident or design, sent a
shock of excitement through her, stirred her to
desire she had not known existed.

But to go out with him on the Common!

To let him touch and take her.

To welcome him in frenzy, an orgasm of a sav-
agery she would not have believed possible: what
could have possessed her but the devil?

She gasped aloud: "But I don't believe in the
devil!" Anguish thickened her voice and she began to sob.

"What did you say, Carol?" It was Police Constable Bessington, standing now by the side of the bed. "Carol, don't cry like that," she went on as if she had caught some of the girl's anguish. "Oh, my dear, don't upset yourself so." She placed her hands on Carol's shoulders to try to steady the girl, but the sobs were convulsive, the strength in the young body quite remarkable. "Stop crying, Carol," she pleaded. "You'll hurt yourself."

Gradually, the girl quietened; and after a while Police Constable Bessington stood back from the narrow bed, and asked again: "What did you say, Carol?"

"I—I didn't say anything," Carol gasped.

"I thought—" the older woman began, and then stopped as if she could not make herself go on. But her eyes were huge as she looked down at the child whose eyelashes were wet with tears, whose cheeks were also streaked with tears, and whose mouth was open and quivering, as if she were fighting back her emotions. Suddenly, the policewoman's voice hardened. "I thought you said 'I don't believe in the devil!'"

Carol gasped: "I don't, I don't, I don't!"

"But why should you say such a thing?" asked Bess, obviously not able to understand.

Carol stared at her. The tears seemed to dry up and her eyes brightened with anger; her lips writhed as she eased herself up on her elbows and cried in a strident voice:

"I must have been possessed of the devil. I must have been!"

Police Constable Bessington recoiled a few inches, then put out both hands, as if to reassure the child. She did not deny or argue, she accepted what Carol had said as if at its face value. There was compassion in her brown eyes but a kind of helplessness, too. Slowly Carol relaxed; as slowly, the older women returned to her place by the bed. She unbuttoned the flap of her tunic pocket and took out a postcard; or what appeared to be be a postcard.

She said: "You were seduced by Lionel, weren't you?"

"I—Oh," Carol gasped. "I—yes. Yes."

"Do you mean *he* was a devil?"

"No," gasped Carol. "No, it dosen't matter. I wish I hadn't told you who it was." She averted her eyes as she went on in a hopeless-sounding voice: 'I'm sorry I'm being so difficult. I—I just want to rest. Please let me rest," she added beseechingly. "Please leave me alone."

"I will, in a few minutes," Bess promised. "The doctor will give you something to help you sleep. But tell me if you know the man in this photograph, Carol. It's very important that we should know."

She did not tell Carol that this photograph was of the dead man found in the clearing at Pucklebury Ring. She did not say that it looked as if this Lionel Willberforce had killed him. She simply turned the postcard over so that Carol could see the photograph. She did not know what she had expected, only knew that it was vital to have the answer to the question. She had not dreamed that the sight of the man in the photograph would upset the girl so much; had not dreamed that it would bring about another paroxysm of crying. Only when the tears had stopped and there was some control, did she hear the anguished girl say:

It's Lionel. You must know it's Lionel. Where—where is he," she gasped. "Why have you got his picture? *Where is he?*"

Police Constable Bessington thought in momentary desperation: How can I tell her that this man is dead, killed by a murderer's hand?

3

Report

As CAROL SMITH stretched herself upon her elbows again, bosom straining against the hospital-issue nightdress, eyes blazing, lips quivering, the door opened and a young-looking doctor came in. He was dusky-skinned, dark-haired with prominent black eyebrows, and had a shadow of stubble on a cleft chin, tufts of dark hair at his ears. Behind him came a nurse. He glanced at the policewoman and motioned to the girl in the bed, who began to scream, saliva spilling from her lips.

"Where is he? Tell me where he is! Why have you got his picture?" She began to scramble off the bed, as if to attack the other woman, and the glitter in her blue eyes was of madness.

The doctor and the nurse acted very quickly.
The doctor got between the patient and the policewoman, the nurse took a small case from her
pocket and opened it, taking out a hypodermic
needle. The doctor held the struggling girl
against him and pushed up the loose sleeve of
the nightdress; the nurse rubbed a patch of
the forearm with a swab pungent with alcohol,
and in less than twenty seconds, the girl had collapsed into unconsciousness. The doctor eased
her away from him and the nurse flattened the
pillows. Between them they straightened Carol's
arms and legs, and soon she lay there with the
sheet up under her chin, peaceful-looking and
free from fear. The nurse pushed the long dark
hair back from the forehead.

"Thank you, Nurse," the doctor said. "I will be
back in the ward very soon." He had a precise
way of talking, not so much an accent as a noticeable intonation. He watched as she collected the
equipment and replaced it in the box, and as
she went out turned to the policewoman. "You
understand of course that I shall have to report
this matter to the authorities. No permission was
given to you or indeed to the police to question
this patient."

Police Constable Bessington, standing up,
looked at him frowning, but in interest rather than
in resentment or dislike.

"Of course you must do whatever you think
right," she said.

"If such a report has repercussions upon you I am sorry," declared the doctor. "But you understand that one's duty is one's duty."

"Doctor," the policewoman responded, "I don't question your right to do what you think best. I don't question mine, either. I thought that it might help the patient. If I was wrong I am sorry." She did not add that she still thought she was right, for there was no point in arguing with this young man; he would, like so many Pakistanis in England—and for all she knew, in Pakistan—abide strictly by the rules. And when Dick Scobie had sent her here he had told her:

"The doctors say no questions. Don't get under their skin, will you?"

Well, she had got under this doctor's skin.

"It is of course easy for all of us to make mistakes," he said. "I, for myself, make many. I will wish you good morning." He bowed slightly, turned and went out.

She stared at the closing door.

There was something quite comical in his pomposity but there was also something likeable in his diffidence and his concern for any repercussions which might affect her. And for his skill and speed she had nothing but admiration. She could not even work herself up into a pitch of indignation because the girl was now unconscious; she doubted whether Carol would have talked reasonably had they not been interrupted. The photograph of Lionel Wilberforce had brought

her emotions to white heat; the emotions of guilt
and fear and pain and, she suspected, love. She
doubted whether she, Bess, would have another
chance to help the girl, even to talk to her. She
had blotted her copybook badly. Smiling wryly,
she sat down and took out her notebook, wrote
down a report of everything that had happened,
including a précis of the conversation with the
doctor, whose name she did not know. One of
the phrases she put down was:

"The patient at one stage of emotional distress
said what I think was: '*I must have been possessed of
the devil. I must have been.*' I tried to make her explain this phrase but she was evasive. At the time
I was not sure that I heard right but I am virtually certain she did use the phrase as quoted."

Another short paragraph read:

"There appears no doubt at all that she went
with Lionel Wilberforce willingly as a lover. I was
unable to find out how much time elapsed between the time he was with her and the time she
became frightened enough to scream. She appears to be badly stricken by remorse."

Bess began to think again.

There were some aspects of this affair which
puzzled her very much, but it did not seem
worthwhile to speculate on paper. At heart she
knew that one of the reasons why she had talked
to the girl was to get results and so make an impression on her superiors. She wanted very
much to be transferred to the Criminal Investi-

gation branch, but she had the good sense to realise that if she elaborated too much in the report she would do herself more harm than good. She finished briefly, closed her book, and was looking across at the girl who looked so young and so angelic, when the door of the little room opened and the nurse who had been here before came in.

"Your relief's on the way," she said. "She's with Sister now." The girl, small and tiny-waisted with huge blue eyes, drew nearer and went on in a conspiratorial whisper. "I'm sorry about Dr. Pataudi, he's such a stickler for the regulations. I heard him talking to Sister. He's a wonderful doctor, and—and, well, there's nothing personal in it, really."

"I'm sure there isn't," Police Constable Bessington answered her. "And thank you."

The nurse looked at the patient and said: "Isn't it an unfair world. Some girls do what she did every night and nothing every goes wrong." There was a long pause before she went on: "And I bet it was her first time."

A minute later, when Elsie Rayburn, her relief, came, Bess was able to hand over with a light heart. She left the hospital thinking: Compassion is a wonderful thing. She was only five minutes' walk from the police station, and was at the end of this tree-lined street when two men came from a gateway. Another was half-concealed by some laurel bushes but she saw the strap round his neck and knew he was a photographer; so these were reporters.

"Is Carol Smith all right?" one of the men asked.

"You know very well that I can't answer any questions," Bess replied sharply.

"Oh, the other reporter protested. "No one would blame you for an incautious word. You've been up all night and must be worn out. *Is* she all right? Was she hurt badly?"

"Did she recognise her assailant?" the second man demanded, and at that moment the photographer stepped from behind the bushes and took three photographs of Bess in quick succession.

Without a word, she walked on.

From the other side of the road a man in a dark brown suit smiled in obvious approval. Bess did not notice him, she was tired and vexed with herself and now angry with the newspapermen who certainly did not come from Halling, for she knew all the local journalists. She went into the big, red-brick, Victorian-built police station, handed in her report, signed off duty and went out. In front of the stone steps was a police car with two uniformed men in it, and one of them leaned across and opened the back door, which swung towards her.

"Jump in, Bess," the driver called. "We'll drop you at home."

She felt a lift of spirits, got in and sank back in

a corner gratefully. Relaxing for the first time, all her muscles seemed to go flabby at once in a surge of utter exhaustion. Neither of the others asked questions, and in five minuutes the car pulled up outside a house in a terrace of houses all built of grey stone, each with a short flight of steps leading up to the front door.

"Have a good sleep, Bess."

"Sleep tight my love."

"Thank you both," she called, and walked to Number 27.

The terrace, Park View, was built in the shape of a shallow crescent, overlooking a small park now empty except for a few elderly people strolling, and one or two mothers pushing prams. Wind rustled through the thick leaves of the trees which fringed the park and made the heads of late tulips nod.

There were four floors in the house, and four bells on the side of the porch, with the name of the flat tenant. Hers was the top flat. She opened the street door with a key and walked up two flights of narrow stairs and one much narrower and steeper. Goodness! How her legs ached! She reached her two-roomed flat at last, and put on a kettle in the tiny kitchen and put out some biscuits. While the kettle was boiling she undressed, slipped on a navy-blue housecoat, then made the tea and sat down, her legs resting on a pouffe.

She thought: I mustn't go to sleep here. I really mustn't. She felt so drowsy. Once, the cup nearly slipped out of her hand. "*I mustn't go to sleep here!*" she told herself, and put the cup down.

A few seconds later she was asleep.

Unlike Woman Police Constable Bessington, Detective Inspector Scobie had been to bed, and slept soundly for five hours, when his plump and pretty wife had woken him, with some resentment, because he was wanted urgently at the station. Half awake, he soothed her as he drank tea, jollied her as he consumed the bacon and eggs which sizzled on his plate, kissed her to breathlessness and then was driven to Halling, recently taken in as a part of Greater London. His was a small, modern, attractive bungalow, five miles from the town centre. In pale sunlight the countryside looked at its best, and in the distance the tall trees this side of Epping Forest showed dark against grassland. Halling, though so near the heart of London, had a character of its own, with a few Tudor buildings, well-preserved, and a great number of gracious and elegant looking Georgian houses, both standing in their own grounds, and in terraces. He drove into the car park behind the police station, one of the ugliest buildings in the town but, blessedly, two blocks off the High Street, and went in the back way.

It was eleven o'clock.

A detective officer came out of the cloakrooms which overlooked the park and Scobie suspected that he had been waiting there for him.

"Good morning, sir!"

"Good morning."

"Quite a morning," the other observed. He was big, fresh-faced, burly, and looked as if he should be wearing a uniform instead of a loose-fitting lounge suit.

"What is that remark supposed to mean?" demanded Scobie.

"Oh, didn't you know, sir? Chief Superintendent Hardy is here from the Yard. Been with the Old Man—the Superintendent, sir—for nearly an hour. *Quite* thought you knew."

"Well, I didn't, but I'm glad to," Scobie rejoined.

At least he had a few minutes in which to adjust to the fact that one of the Metropolitan Police Force's most celebrated senior officers was here: this was why he had been summoned. The Superintendent of the Halling Division hadn't said so, the old fox. He must be in his fifties, but he hadn't cured himself of the habit of springing surprises, as if he believed part of his mission in life was to catch his subordinates on the wrong foot. Scobie turned into his own small office which overlooked the parking place and the ugly brick structure of a cinema which had been built between the wars. His desk, as always, was im-

maculately tidy. On top of a file marked: *New
Material* was a typewritten note from one of the
detective sergeants:

1. The Superintendent called for a copy of a
   report as detailed as practicable on the
   Carol Smith-Lionel Wilberforce case. I had
   all your notes copied on the photo-copy
   m/c and the originals sent to the Super's
   office.
2. The Superintendent and Chief Det. S.
   Hardy called for the report from W.P.C.
   Bessington and there was no time to get a
   copy made. I sent the original in, sir.
3. W.P.C.B. appears to have dropped a brick
   at the hospital.
4. Cause of death of Lionel Wilberforce:
   manual strangulation. Provisional autopsy
   report promised by 3 p.m. today.
5. Carol Smith, daughter of the Patriarch at
   Merryfield Community, now under sedation. Understand she made no official
   statement before medical authorities insisted on putting her under sedation.
6. The London newspapers are at us all the
   time. W.P.C.B. was accosted and photo-
   graphed on the way from the hospital but
   made no comment.

                              J.R.S. Det. Sergeant.

Scobie sat at his desk and read these notes
through several times until he virtually knew

them off by heart. He was sitting back and looking out of the window when his inter-office telephone rang. He picked it up quickly and said:

"Scobie."

"Come and see me at once," Superintendent Atkinson ordered.

"Right, sir!" Scobie replaced the receiver as briskly as he spoke, and went out of the room immediately. Atkinson's office was a big corner room with a large bay window in one corner; a kind of turret room. He was sitting at his huge flat-topped desk with five steel filing-cabinets behind him set against a wall covered with photographs of police football, cricket and athletic teams, unique in the Metropolitan Police. The other walls were hung with charts, one showing the ranking of the Criminal Investigation Department in the Force, another showing the complement in this division of Halling.

Atkinson sat behind the desk, fat as a Buddha with two chins. He wore an immaculate dark suit, his flabby features relieved only by the sharpness of his periwinkle blue eyes. He had very little hair, but it was brushed over his pate to make the most of it, like a pale gold sheen.

Standing by the side of the desk was Chief Superintendent Hardy, silver-haired, clean-shaven, a little on the plump side but not really fat. He had blue eyes, too; and good features: a distinguished-looking man whom Scobie had seen only two or three times, then at a distance.

Sitting in a wooden armchair was another, older man with long, silky hair and a long, beautifully kept moustache. His face was vaguely familiar but at that moment Scobie was much more concerned with the two senior policemen and gave the older man little more than a glance.

"Good morning, sir," he said to Atkinson, and then to Hardy: "Sir."

"Good morning."

"Morning," grunted Atkinson, and tapped a shorthand notebook on his desk. The question he was about to ask was meant to be disconcerting, another habit he had developed so as to keep his men on their toes. "Woman Police Constable Bessington. How reliable is she? Is she fanciful? Imaginative, I mean? What do you think of her?"

Scobie, half-warned by the notes from J.R.S., pursed his lips, paused long enough to make it clear that his reply was considered, and then replied:

"She is a reliable, thoughtful, painstaking officer and very well-respected, sir. As for fanciful—I shouldn't think so. She does a great deal of work among young women in need of care and attention—in fact that's one reason why she joined the Force. Her husband was killed when a bridge collapsed in Wales about two years ago, and until then she'd done a lot of voluntary welfare work. I don't know whether you could call her imaginative. Understanding is more the word I would use."

"Understanding of what?" demanded Atkinson. "Her job? Instructions? She appears to have defied an instruction not to question Carol Smith. Is it her habit to do what she wants? Is she headstrong? Hardly a recommendation to the C.I.D. if she is."

4

Dr. Cellini

SCOBIE FELT HOT under the collar, and hoped that his feelings did not show. Atkinson always had a tendency to show off, to make one look small, but this hectoring manner was worse than usual; something must have got badly under his skin. Now he appeared to glare, and had one clenched fist on the desk, as if to bang it exhortingly. But he did not move it, simply waited.

"I don't know what happened, sir," Scobie said quietly. "It's possible that she simply used initiative. I've always encouraged the use of initiative in officers on whose judgment I felt I could rely." When Atkinson didn't answer he went on doggedly: "I think she is a very good candidate for the Criminal Investigation Department, and could be wasted if she is simply used on street patrols and the general uniform duties."

Hardy interpolated: "We can certainly use able women officers, Inspector."

"What *did* go wrong, sir?" Scobie asked Atkinson.

"Apparently she questioned the witness in such a way that it brought about an attack of hysteria, and the girl had to be placed under sedation. We can't hope to question her for the rest of the day."

"May I ask who reported this, sir?"

"The hospital authorities."

"Do you know which individual?" asked Scobie doggedly.

"That is hardly a question which need concern you," Atkinson said coldly. "We can get W.P.C. Bessington's version of the incident later. Have you seen her report?"

"No, sir." What the devil was the matter with the man? He must know that he, Scobie, hadn't had a chance to look at the notebook now on his desk. Scobie felt more incensed than ever and looked hard into his superior's eyes; to look away might create an impression of weakness.

"Did you talk to the witness, Carol Smith?"

"No, sir." Why call her a witness instead of a victim of assault? Scobie wondered.

"Did you have any opportunity?"

"No," answered Scobie. "She was in the ambulance when I arrived on the scene. Police Constable Dimitry had acted promptly and resuscitated her, but she was very dazed if not unconscious. I thought it wise not to attempt to question her in that condition."

The man in the chair moved but did not speak. The window was open, and wind stirred white hair which looked like spun silk. Hardy, standing until then, took an upright chair, Scobie wondered what he thought of this interview; whether this was the way he would have conducted it himself. He, Scobie, was more resigned to the situation now, even though he could not understand what had affected Atkinson so.

"Did she *say* anything in your hearing?" Atkinson wanted to know.

"No, sir."

"Or in the hearing of the policeman who first arrived on the scene?"

"Not as far as I know," answered Scobie. He found the impulse to ask what had happened almost irresistible, but knew that he had to restrain himself; and Atkinson would surely come to the point soon. "I asked all the men, four in all, whether she had said anything to indicate her attacker or said anything at all, and they assured me they had heard nothing. Dimitry went on foot, the others responded by patrol car to his first call for help. I even asked Clipper Dee if he had heard her say anything."

"Clipper Dee?" Hardy asked, as if startled. "Was he involved?"

The question did much to restore Scobie's good humour. It showed beyond doubt that Hardy was in touch with events in the division as well as at Scotland Yard. Dee was hardly a renowned criminal, but he had been twice convicted of robbery, and sentenced first to six months and then to a year's imprisonment. His method was to mark down a youngish middle-aged woman who would be flattered by the attentions of a younger man, seduce her, and after a while wheedle money out of her. The development of this made the crime: he had taken keys from two women and used these keys to enter their flats and take whatever articles he could sell easily. To make sure the flats were empty, he first telephoned his lady-loves and made an appointment far enough away to be sure he wasn't disturbed.

Scobie had arrested him in Halling for the second offence over two years ago.

And the great Superintendent Hardy was familiar with his name!

All of these things flashed through Scobie's mind before he answered: "He's not involved in this affair as far as I can find out, sir. He was on the Common having fun, and this time he was with a young girl who hasn't two pennies to rub together, so I don't see what he could have wanted except a night or two on the tiles."

"Then how does he come in?" asked Hardy.

"He helped P.C. Dimitry look for the girl who

screamed," Scobie answered. "So did two others, but they vanished as soon as she'd been found."

"I see," Hardy said, turning to Atkinson, whose neck was so fat and stiff that he had difficulty in turning it. "When can we see P.C. Dimitry?"

For the first time, the man in the chair spoke, in a gentle voice with a trace of accent; he enunciated with great lucidity of tone and expression, all the same.

"And, perhaps, Woman Police Constable Bessington. Is that possible?" he was asking Atkinson, and appeared to be slightly over-deferential. He had very clear grey eyes and a soft, pinkish skin and complexion: like a moustachioed cherub. As Scobie looked at him, recognition dawned. This was Dr. Emmanuel Cellini, the psychiatrist, a man who was often consulted by the police, and as often by the defence, in major trials. He had featured in more *causes célèbres* than anyone else in recent years, and his reputation could hardly have been more distinguished.

Recognition distracted Scobie from pleading that Police Constable Bessington had only just gone off duty. He had sent her to the hospital although she had been due to go off duty at twelve o'clock, because he had thought her the most likely policewoman to make the Smith girl talk.

Without looking at Scobie, Atkinson said: "We can send for both whenever you like, Doctor."

As if only suddenly remembering that the two
men hadn't been introduced, he went on: "This
is Dr. Cellini, Inspector—Dr. Emmanuel
Cellini."

"I'm very glad to meet you, sir," Scobie said.

"Thank you," replied Cellini. "Thank you very
much. I wonder—" he looked tentatively from
Atkinson to Hardy. "I wonder if Inspector
Scobie were to see the policewoman's report
whether it would enable him to help us even
more." Before Atkinson could answer, the
white-haired man gave a deprecating smile and
went on: "Perhaps I should explain that I have
been consulted quite recently, within the last two
days in fact—by Mr. Joshua Smith, the man who
is called the Patriarch at the Merryfield Community, and whose daughter is now in this distressing plight. Indeed," went on Cellini as if it did
not occur to him that he was usurping Atkinson's
right to inform Scobie, "I had told Superintendent Hardy of this consultation and when early
this morning he heard that Carol Smith was involved, he telephoned me. I cannot thank you
enough, Mr. Atkinson, for your readiness to let
me sit in, and your discretion in keeping the
name of the young woman, as well as that of the
murdered man, from the newspapers. The
Merryfield Community will be inundated with
newspapermen the moment the names *are* released. I suspect that more Fleet Street reporters
than usual have already shown great interest,

possibly because the scene of a rumoured raping and killing was so close to the Community."

Cellini stopped, and Scobie thought that the words of the white-haired psychiatrist, so calm-sounding and considered, had in fact opened up a vast new field of speculation and enquiry: a serious one, even a grave one, or V.I.P. Hardy would not have come here with him.

Atkinson pushed across a sparsely-typed report and Scobie read everything that Police Constable Bessington had listed: A detailed précis of her interview with Carol. As he handed the report back, Atkinson spoke over his "Thank you."

"Have you noticed more Fleet Street reporters than usual? Your friend Clipper Dee would not be slow in selling them a story."

"I've been told there are several about," answered Scobie. "And a story of murder following rape would be enough to attract them, surely." He straightened up. "If the Press knew just what we've got on our hands with the added twist that it is the rapist or seducer who was murdered, they'd come swarming, sir. They simply don't know yet, so my friend Dee hasn't sold his story to anyone. He'd wait in any case, guessing that he'll get more when the case really breaks." Excitement almost carried Scobie away, but he checked himself. "Shall I fetch Bessington and Dimitry, sir?"

"Can't you send for them?"

"Just as you like," said Scobie, and went on in a more relaxed manner: "but I really think they should be warned that it isn't routine, and also be warned what it's about. They would have time to search their memories on the way here if they're told in advance."

Atkinson was staring as if prepared to say no. Scobie waited, standing stiffly, Cellini moved to the window and looked out, and Hardy, obviously sensing tension between these two men, did not aggravate it by making any comment. At last, Atkinson waved a fat hand.

"All right, go and get them yourself. But don't be long. We have a lot to do."

"I would so much like to see the place where the crimes were committed," said Cellini gently. "But I would like to see these two young officers first, if I may."

"They live within two miles of each other," Scobie said. "And I'll have my sergeant telephone them to make sure we don't waste any time." He turned and went out briskly, still not sure why Cellini was here. He thrust open the door of his office and elderly Detective Sergeant James Richard Shepherd looked up from his desk. "Call Bessington and young Dimitry and tell them I'm going to collect them in the next ten or fifteen minutes and bring them here, will you?" He closed the door on Shepherd and went striding along the passage. In the main hall were five men, including two photographers, and as soon as he appeared, they began to call out:

"Can you give us a statement, Inspector?"

"Who is the girl at the hospital?"

"*Was* she raped?"

"And what's this about the murdered man? Did he come from Merryfield?"

Scobie, at the foot of the stairs, made a quick assessment of the group, knowing that it would be folly to antagonise them. He forced a smile and said: "There's a conference of V.I.P.s up with Superintendent Atkinson now. If I let any cats out of the bag *my* life won't be worth living. You know Chief Superintendent John Hardy's there, don't you?"

A man called: "Why do you think *we're* here?"

Someone else asked in a keen voice: "Is it true that Manny Cellini is here, too?"

"You really will have to check with the Superintendent," Scobie replied. "And I have to go and make sure what's happening at Pucklebury Ring. I'll see you." With a wave of his hand he hurried through the rear of the station to the car park. To his surprise, no one followed him: they probably thought that his talk of Pucklebury Ring was a red herring.

Dimitry lived on the far side of the Common and the shortest route to his home was across it, skirting the Ring. As he drew nearer, Scobie saw a crowd of at least a hundred people, including a

dozen or so women with babies in prams. A few
dogs were roaming. A smooth-haired terrier on
a lead was snapping at a golden retriever. Several police cars stood about and a large area of
the Ring itself had been cordoned off with white
rope strung around trees. Within this area, the
girl had been attacked and the man had been
killed. Scobie had a word with another detective
inspector, who was in charge, then drove to the
far side of the Common. When he reached the
road, he could see, among the trees, some of the
buildings of the Merryfield Community. The entrance was off a by-road, a mile away. Some half
mile to the left was a new estate of reasonably
good houses, all privately owned. Two different
new sites were being cleared for fresh building.
This was the Halling Garden Estate, a community of some two hundred families each of which
had its own box of a house or bungalow and its
pleasant patch of garden back and front, a garage and a white-painted wooden fence to keep
it separate from its neighbours.

Dimitry lived in one of the bungalows.

His motor-cycle was in the open garage next to
a mini-car which he seldom used himself, but
kept for his wife and family; there were three
children, Scobie knew. He left the car outside
and walked to the front of the house, and as he
drew near he heard a woman speaking in an angry, low-pitched voice:

"Hero? Some bloody hero *you* are! Not to me,

anyhow, and not to the kids. How can you be a hero to your kids if you never see them?" Dimitry made no reply and after a pause the woman went on: "If I want you to take me out shopping, oh no, you're too bloody tired, but if Mr. Flicking Scobie snaps his finger you can't get off quick enough."

Dimitry said patiently: "That's enough, Anne. He'll be here in a minute and he wouldn't come himself if it wasn't important."

"What you've got to decide is whether *I'm* more important than the Police Force, or whether you're married to the flicking coppers."

"Pack it in, Anne—" Dimitry began.

Scobie put a hand on the door bell and gave a long push; he could hear the ringing sound some distance away. Both voices fell silent. Scobie waited, whistling only just above his breath. Soon, footsteps came thumping down a flight of stairs and the door was pulled open. Young Dimitry—he was nearly thirty but still looked like a fresh-faced, curly-haired boy— appeared, uniform on and helmet in hand.

"Hallo, sir!"

"Hallo, Constable," Scobie said in a carrying voice. "We need to have a first-hand report of that job you did last night." He led the way, Dimitry following eagerly and putting on his helmet. It seemed to add not only six inches to his height but ten years to his age. He did not call back to his wife, which probably indicated his

mood. As he got into the car, Scobie saw Mrs.
Dimitry at the window, an attractive woman who
looked more Italian or Southern European than
English, although her speech was unmistakably
native. He could see that she was scowling. A
man who liked to know all he could about those
who worked with him, Scobie understood the
debilitating effect that an unhappy marriage
could have on a man's work and so on his career;
but this wasn't the time to talk about Dimitry's
domestic life.

"We're going to collect Constable Bessington,"
Scobie said. "I'll brief you both after we've
picked her up."

Dimitry said heavily: "Thank you, sir. It's about
last night, I suppose."

"Yes. We shall probably attempt a reconstruc-
tion," Scobie told him. "In any case the Superintendent as well as Chief Superintendent Hardy
from Scotland Yard want all possible details. We
have to make sure that nothing's overlooked."

After a pause, Dimitry said: "There isn't much
that I saw and heard that I didn't tell you about,
sir. But I'll do all I can."

"I'm sure you will," Scobie said reassuringly.

When he turned into Park View he saw Bess
waiting for him, and although the glassiness of
her tired eyes showed when they drew up, she
was as brisk as ever when she opened the car
door and got in next to Scobie. Two or three
times she turned in her seat to look at Dimitry

but Scobie saw nothing significant in that. He told them all he could, emphasised the need to remember every detail and every word, even every intonation of speech, and had no doubt that each was fully briefed before they reached Divisional Headquarters. Forty-five minutes from the time he had left, Scobie was back at Superintendent Atkinson's room, knowing everything that either of his companions could tell him. He opened the door at a summons, thought Cellini said "Speak of the devil" and was mildly surprised, and then said:

"Both Dimitry and Bessington are here, sir."

"Good," Cellini said. "You have been very quick." There was obviously both eagerness and excitement in his eyes, while Hardy stood by as if interested but certainly not excited. Atkinson's Buddha-like face held an expression of sheer disbelief.

Disbelief of what? Scobie wondered.

"Bring them both in," said Atkinson, in a voice which seemed to add: "And let's put an end to this nonsense."

Scobie opened the door wider and first Bess and then Dimitry stepped inside.

5

"Family Party"

WOMAN POLICE CONSTABLE BESSINGTON thought: There's something very strange going on here. It was clearly apparent in Atkinson's expression, even in the fact that his face was pink-tinged; it was almost as if all three of them in the room had been quarrelling and been forced to break off abruptly. She sensed that Scobie was aware of the strain, too. The Scotland Yard man looked pleasant enough. She had heard a great deal about him and yet had never met him before. At times she seemed to have been in the Police Force forever: at others, she felt as if she knew hardly anything about it, and this was one of those moments.

Then she saw and recognised Cellini, and

sight of him went through her like an electric
shock. In fact she simply stood and stared, being so taken aback. She did not know of a
human being for whom she had a greater
regard, and knew of many social workers who
shared her feeling of veneration. She was
aware of Atkinson, who mumbled introductions:
"Woman Police Constable Bessington . . . Police
Constable Dimitry . . . Chief Superintendent
Hardy . . . Dr. Cellini." Atkinson still looked
pink and shaken and there was a rasp of anger in
his voice.

Cellini looked at Bess, and she was sure he
recognised her. He moved towards her with his
hand outstretched.

"How very good to see you again," he said. "I
had no idea you had joined the Police Force."

His grip was firm and cool.

"My husband died," Bess said.

"I am very sorry," replied Cellini. "But glad at
least that you are putting your life to such good
purpose."

She felt Atkinson's gaze on her, disapproving,
and glimpsed Hardy's look of surprise. Her own
face changed colour; it was a long time since she
had blushed so deeply. In those few minutes she
wasn't very clear about what was said, except
that Dimitry was now answering questions about
what he had heard and seen. This was really the
first time she had heard exactly what had started
this investigation; she hadn't even known that he

had saved Carol Smith with the kiss of life. She watched him with new interest as she listened. He was a strong-looking, handsome man with a very firm chin, and a pleasant voice which, at the moment, sounded nervous. Now and again his voice went dry. He described exactly what he had heard, done and seen, standing at attention in front of Atkinson and the huge desk.

At last, he finished, gulped, and moved back a pace.

"And that's everything?" Atkinson demanded.

"Everything I recall, sir," stated Dimitry, "and I've been over it in my mind time and time again."

"The slightest sound or movement or word could be of great importance," Atkinson barked.

"I understand, sir," Dimitry answered stiffly. What on earth is the matter with the Chief? Bess asked herself. She thought that Hardy, who had been remarkably quiet, was looking at Atkinson with disapproval, and the tension she had sensed on arrival seemed to worsen; it affected everyone. Before Atkinson or the others commented, this was broken by a sharp ring of one of the three telephones on Atkinson's desk. Atkinson snatched it up and barked:

"Chief Superintendent? *Who*? . . . Oh." His change of tone was comical, the way he looked at Hardy was one of bafflement. He gulped much as Dimitry had. "It's the Commander," he said, in a hollow voice. "For you."

"Ah." Hardy said. "Thank you." He took the

receiver, while each of the others stared at him
with varying degrees of interest. "Hardy here,
sir," he said into the telephone. "Yes . . . Yes . . .
I wonder if you will hold on while I get to another telephone. Won't be a jiffy." He put the receiver on the desk and said: "This is confidential,
Superintendent. Where can I take the call? No,
no," he went on as Atkinson started up. "I don't
want to drive you all out of the office."

"There's my room close by," Scobie volunteered.

"Yes, that'll do—Scobie's room. I'll take you,"
Atkinson agreed and moved cumbersomely
from his desk while Scobie, nearest the door,
opened it for the two Superintendents to go out.
On his feet, Atkinson, a tall man, was enormous.
The floor shook. Atkinson's voice sounded
clearly, Hardy's was a murmur. A door closed
and in a moment or two Atkinson was on his way
back; he didn't come in but went instead into the
cloakroom next door. That door closed with a
bang, too.

Bess thought, something's really worrying the
Old Man. The others must be aware of it but
none spoke until Cellini moved to her and began
to talk in a most natural way about her husband
and her past. Both she and Clive had been voluntary workers on the Probation Service of a
London borough, and one of the girls in their
charge had been murdered.

"I remember the case vividly," Cellini said in

his gentle voice. "Her sister killed her, the sister whom everyone believed was so good and compassionate."

Bess said simply: "But the one who was really good and compassionate was you, of course."

"Now, come, my dear," Cellini waved his hands in disclaimer, but he was manifestly pleased. He drew Scobie and Dimitry into the conversation which he turned towards Merryfield, but he did not once mention Carol Smith or the dead man, Lionel Wilberforce. Bess thought: It's almost as if Wilberforce didn't exist, as if all I can think about is the girl.

Her thoughts changed as Atkinson came to the office from one direction and Hardy from the other.

Chief Detective Superintendent John Hardy was now the senior Chief Superintendent at Scotland Yard, where he had worked for nearly twenty-five years. For much of this time he had known the present Commander C.I.D., who was at least as much friend as colleague; and both had known Manny Cellini for many years. For that matter, they had both known Atkinson, too. As he walked from the big room to Scobie's smaller one, Hardy speculated on Atkinson's attitude; once he was shut in the office alone, he did more than speculate; he took action.

"I didn't want Atkinson to hear this," he said. "But I'd like Manny to have an hour with the three officers involved, on their own. One at a time or all together, as Manny thinks best. So if you are coming to have a look yourself—"

"I am," the Commander interpolated.

"Then supposing I bring Atkinson to meet you at the place where it happened," Hardy said.

"I don't know what you're up to," said the Commander, "but that's all right with me."

"And if I'm called away—" began Hardy.

"I've no doubt we could manage without you while you have your *tête-à-tête* with Manny," the Commander said, and added with a change of tone: "Afterwards, you will have a *tête-à-tête* with me."

"Yes, sir," Hardy replied with mock humility. He put down the receiver, pondering as he went out slowly. He noticed that a door at the end of this passage was open, and saw it open wider for Atkinson to squeeze through; he caught a glimpse of a W.C. pedestal and guessed that the Divisional man had been lurking there to meet him when he appeared. Atkinson beckoned and moved a few yards along the passage, and as Hardy joined him, lowered his voice and asked:

"I don't know Dr. Cellini very well, John. Do you? *Is* he all right. Don't have very much time for psychiatrists generally, you know."

"You can rely on Manny Cellini," Hardy assured him. "He is not a Freudian fanatic or a specialist in mumbo-jumbo, or anywhere near it. Reggie, how far away is Halling Common?"

"You mean where the murder took place? Only ten minutes or so—why?"

"The Commander wants to meet us there, and I would like to have a look at the spot first. Never wise to be caught with half a story. Take me over there and show me round, will you? Then we'll go to this Community place and see what's on," Hardy added. "Presumably you've seen the girl's father."

Atkinson said gruffly: "No. Not yet. Wanted to get the dead man identified first. Now according to the girl he's one of the Community—*now's* the time to talk to Smith. He's been to the hospital but his daughter was still unconscious."

"Is he aware that Wilberforce is dead?"

"Not as far as I know," Atkinson answered. "I gave no instructions."

"I see," Hardy said, and after a few moments he went on: "Well, after we've been to Merryfield, if you know of a really good place to lunch in Halling, we'll take the Commander there. He's a great one for food."

"No greater than I, I'll wager," Atkinson boasted, with obvious satisfaction. "I know just the place. Want to get off right away?"

"Please."

"What about Dr. Cellini—" Atkinson began.

"If you'll just tell anyone we see to answer any questions he puts to them, that will do the trick," Hardy assured him. "He'll keep it under his hat."

"I certainly hope you're right," Atkinson said.
He pushed the other door open wider and made
his pronouncement, sweeping the room with
what was no doubt intended to be a commanding glance. "Give Dr. Cellini all the help he re-
quires," he boomed. "Answer his questions as
freely as you would answer mine—or Chief Superintendent Hardy's," he added hastily. "We
are going to the scene of the crime." He nodded,
smiled stiffly at Cellini, and went out, closing the
door firmly.

Outside in the street, the number of Fleet
Street newspapermen had grown to at least a
dozen. Cameras flashed and questions were
hurled, but all Hardy said was: "There'll be an
official statement later. I'm going to the place
where it happened, now."

There was a rush of men to parked cars and
seven or eight engines seemed to splutter and
growl at once.

Emmanuel Cellini turned from the door of
the big office as Atkinson went out, and looked
up at Scobie, straight-faced. Scobie closed the
door. Cellini, life-trained to sense atmosphere,
knew that these three people were much, much
lighter of spirit than they had been for a long
time; the woman even looked less tired. Dimitry
was glancing at her, and waves of some kind of
understanding reached Cellini. Dimitry had a
classically handsome face, was an Apollo of a

man, and the woman had the same kind of classic look although her features were thinner. She was too thin, he thought; given another ten pounds or so she would be magnificent.

Dimitry turned away from contemplation of her almost guiltily.

"I wonder if we could get some coffee, or tea," said Cellini. "And is there a smaller room—yours, perhaps, Inspector?"

Soon, they were sitting round Scobie's desk drinking coffee and eating biscuits from a plate piled with them, from semi-sweet to sandwich, from plain wafer to rich chocolate-covered. Bless John Hardy for his quick understanding of the need to get Atkinson away! He must have a word with John about the fat man's physical condition, but for the moment he had these three with him and knew exactly what he expected to get from them. He led into conversation about the case with a passing reference to Dimitry's resuscitation.

"How long have you been able to give the kiss of life, Adam?"

"Oh, a long time, sir."

"In a way you are a lucky man to have been able to use it actually to save a life," Cellini remarked: "Don't you think so, Bess?" When she nodded, Cellini went on: "What I would very much like to know is *exactly* what you heard and saw, Adam. I know you must be tired of repeating it, but Superintendent Atkinson is right, you know, a trifle can be of vital importance. Quite vital. And there is at least one very peculiar aspect of the case—the man who presumably seduced this Carol and later made her scream, himself being found dead of strangulation near the scene of his own crime."

"We don't know for certain that he was the man who attacked the girl," objected Scobie. "Only that she thinks he was. There's a lot of confusion in her mind—or there was at the time of your talk with her, Bess."

"What did the girl say when you showed her the photograph?" Cellini asked Bess.

"She just cried out 'It's Lionel'," Bess answered. "She seemed to think I knew it must be Lionel and wanted to know why I had the photograph. She went into hysteria, that was why I got into trouble with Dr. Pataudi." Bess paused but went on without prompting: "I really don't understand. She behaved as if Lionel mattered desperately to her, whereas a girl who had been nearly killed by a man doesn't usually yell—" Bess broke off.

"That's what I mean," Scobie put in.

"She certainly screamed as if she thought he was killing her," Dimitry said.

"How often *did* she scream?" asked Scobie.

"Half-a-dozen times, I suppose. It was a broken sound part of the time—like this," Dimitry placed his fingers on his neck, just above the Adam's apple, and gave a choked scream, removed his fingers so that the sound blasted out: "*Eeeek!*" and then pressed again until there was hardly any sound at all. "It was as if the chap was choking her and she kept freeing herself and screaming, until he caught her again. You have to be a maniac to choke the life out of a girl you've just made love to."

When Dimitry stopped, all three waited for more. Inwardly Cellini was very pleased that they were talking so freely and naturally: this was the atmosphere and the frame of mind which could evoke unremembered trifles.

"Why should she scream if she wasn't attacked?" demanded Dimitry.

"She could suddenly have realised what she'd done," Bess said, and went on: "Could—" she broke off, looking at Scobie.

"Could what?" asked Scobie.

"Could you possibly—" Bess began again; and she stopped again. Then she asked: "How was Lionel Wilberforce killed?"

"Manual strangulation," Scobie answered.

"Had he had intercourse?"

"Well," said Scobie, "his trousers were unfastened, and—"

"I have seen the autopsy report," put in Cellini, "and there is no doubt at all that he had had an orgasm shortly before his death."

"Why—" Bess began.

"Why what?" asked Cellini.

"Why on earth should he be so savage with a

girl who went with him willingly and then get up
and run away before he's done up his fly?" asked
Bess. "It doesn't seem to make any sense."

"Unless *he* was scared," Dimitry remarked.

"Couldn't be any other explanation," said
Scobie. "He must have known or discovered that
someone else was there, rolled off the girl and
scrambled away. Or tried to," he added grimly.
"Whoever interrupted the pretty little scene
soon caught up with him—my God!"

"Good heavens!" exclaimed Bess.

"How dumb can you be?" gasped Dimitry. "It
wasn't Wilberforce who tried to strangle her, it
was this other chap. He must have been nearby
all the time. Must have been! He must have seen
what happened or soon caught up with them
and—" He broke off, his expression changing, as
if suddenly he had been deflated.

"Whom did he attack first?" Bess said.

That's it, that's it, Cellini enthused within himself. Keep prodding, young Dimitry.

"How could it have been the girl first?" asked
Scobie.

"I don't understand you," retorted Dimitry.
"I—oh, I see! *I* heard the screams and started
out within seconds, but I didn't hear any sound
of scuffling, or running. I heard the men who
came to help me, that's all. It looks as if the assailant killed Wilberforce and then—"

"And then attacked Carol," Bess put in
eagerly.

"Hardly possible," amended Scobie. "Let's see what we know for fact. The girl screamed. She had had intercourse, on her evidence, with Wilberforce, who didn't scream. The lab people can no doubt check whether these two actually had intercourse with each other. Can't they, sir?" He consulted Cellini.

"Yes," Cellini said. "Yes, I think several ways, but that isn't immediately important, is it?"

"Damned important and at this very minute," Dimitry answered for Scobie. "If they did make love together, then Wilberforce was killed after the act, and his killer could have been the one who tried to strangle her. If they didn't—oh, that makes it too confusing."

"The girl has already told me she and Wilberforce made love," Bess said wryly. "That's where I came unstuck, in trying to make her talk more." She gave a little laugh. "I don't know who else keeps falling into this trap but I keep forgetting Lionel Wilberforce—"

"Bess," interrupted Scobie, "there's one thing you can tell us better than anyone else. If Carol had an orgasm, and if it was her first, would she—or could she—have been so dazed for a minute or two afterwards that she was unaware of what was going on? Could Wilberforce have moved from her, for instance, and another man started to choke her, without her realising that it wasn't the same man?"

"Knowing the mood Carol was in, the sudden

onslaught of remorse, *and* knowing how utterly
exhausting an orgasm can be, especially—" Bess
broke off, only to add: "Yes, I think so. Don't
you, Dr. Cellini?"

"I do indeed," Cellini answered.

"I keep forgetting Wilberforce was murdered
and that we have to trace his murderer. Does
anyone know if there are any traces of the man
who escaped? It's as if he were spirited away,"
she went on, and added angrily: "But that's
nonsense!"

After a pause which seemed to last for a long
time, Cellini said: "Is it, Bess?"

That was the first time since they had been together in this room that the others all turned towards him, distracted by the question which
must have sounded absurd.

6

Talk of the Devil

"I DON'T UNDERSTAND you," Bess said.

"You can't be serious," said Dimitry.

"What are you driving at?" asked Scobie, in a sharp voice.

"I asked Bess a simple question," said Cellini, smiling. He pushed back the ends of his elegant moustache with the forefinger of his right hand, and revealed full, pink, well-shaped lips. "Bess, you said it was as if this man who killed Wilberforce was spirited away, didn't you? And before anyone of us could comment you dismissed the idea as nonsense!"

Bess said slowly: "Yes."

"But it *is* nonsense!" exclaimed Dimitry.

Scobie sat back in his own office chair and

watched Cellini closely. Nothing this man said
could be dismissed as nonsense, so there must be
something in his mind. The room was very still.
Sun glinted on the empty coffee cups and on the
pewter pot and pewter jug in which coffee and
milk had been served. Only a few crumbs and a
corner of a biscuit were on the plate which had
been so full. On the roof by the window pigeons
sat in the sun and cooed. Now and again footsteps sounded on the parking areas, an engine
roared and a car moved in or out. Now and
again also, a man walked along the passage outside Scobie's door, but none paused to come in.
Dimitry was catching the sun on one side of his
face. He looked like a Greek god.

"Bess," Cellini said coaxingly. "why did you
say it was as if the man were spirited away?"

"I don't really know," Bess muttered, and
added: "I wish to goodness I hadn't."

"Think," urged Cellini. "And don't be afraid
of saying what you think, my dear. Nothing is so
absurd as believing that what one thinks without
understanding why is necessarily absurd. It
stands to reason that all thoughts are subcon-
scious in the beginning so all words have some
kind of motivation."

"But really—" began Dimitry, with a touch of
impatience, and he would have gone on but for
the pressure of Bess's hand on his arm. He took
the hint at once.

"And I would simply like to know why you

said what you did," went on Cellini. "What do *you* think prompted you?"

Bess said quietly: "The disappearance seems so uncanny."

"Uncanny?"

"Well, *does* what happened make sense?" demanded Bess. "The seduction, the change from ecstasy to horror, the murder of the man who might or might not have tried to kill Carol. How can we make reason out of it?"

"The one certain thing is that there *is* reason," Cellini said. "Or at least, an explanation. Can you think of anything else which might have prompted you to say that it was almost as if he were spirited away?"

Very slowly, almost painfully, Bess said: "Yes."

"Please tell us," pleaded Cellini.

"It—it's probably fancy, perhaps just a play on words," Bess told him, "and I think I mis-heard Carol Smith. It—it's very hard to explain," she went on hesitantly. "I can remember the words but I can't really tell you how I felt or how she looked. She seemed—haunted. Terrified. And I could swear she said: '*I must have been possessed of the devil.*' I put that in my report," Bess added, hurriedly. "I wondered whether I should, but somehow I couldn't help myself. It was almost as if—" She broke off, and raised her hands in a gesture of bewilderment. "Almost as if someone was making me."

Cellini exuded a long, slow: "*Aahhh.*"

"Bess—" began Dimitry, and stopped.

"If we go on like this you'll have me believing in ghosts," Scobie said, half-seriously.

"You don't have to believe in ghosts to believe in the secret voices," retorted Cellini. "We all have them and at some time or other we all hear them. Some talk about conscience, some talk about telepathy, some talk of being possessed."

"By the devil," Bess said huskily.

"Even if she did say it," Dimitry remarked intently, "she must have meant Wilberforce turned into a kind of devil."

"Is that what you think?" Scobie asked Bess.

She looked not at him but at Cellini, who sat absolutely still. His hands, open, were held towards her encouragingly. He was not smiling but his eyes were very bright and eager: expectant in a way it was difficult to understand.

"No," she replied with reluctant honesty. "I think she felt she had been possessed of the devil when she allowed Wilberforce to seduce her. By evil, if you like. By—Satan." When Dimitry caught his breath as if to protest, she went on, her gaze concentrated on Cellini. "Of course it's nonsense, no one is possessed of the devil, we don't believe in that superstition any more. But she sounded as if *she* meant it. She sounded— bruised, broken, spiritually hurt more than she could bear. And helpless and hopeless, too. You see, she felt and she behaved as if she were terribly ashamed. She told me she thought she must

be a harlot because she went out with a man who
belonged to another woman. She—"

"Belonged?" asked Cellini sharply.

"In this day and age!" exclaimed Dimitry.

"She knew he was married in the sense they
use marriage at the Merryfield Community,"
went on Bess. "They believe in the exclusivism of
two people who give themselves to each other.
They have much more rigid sexual moral
standards than I had realised. And she felt she
had betrayed the Community as well as the other
woman. That was as if she had betrayed herself."

After a pause, Cellini said: "Bess."

"Yes, Doctor?"

"You are quite sure of these things?"

"Absolutely."

"She felt terribly ashamed because she had betrayed others and herself?"

"Yes," Bess agreed.

"Then unarguably she did go willingly with
this man."

"That's what I can't understand," said Bess,
looking round desperately. "That's the only reason I would think seriously that there might
have been another man there. Oh, if only I'd the
skill to make her talk before that damned doctor
interrupted."

"As we have seen, there could have been an attacker after the seducer," said Cellini firmly.

"I've always thought there was another man,"
Scobie began.

"He wouldn't have had *time!*" Dimitry's voice rose at the last word.

"There is the possibility which Bess has already accepted," contributed Cellini gently. "That after the moments of ecstasy she was in a kind of trance, and on waking from this was obviously overcome by a terrible remorse. In that remorse she could have become so hysterical that she became confused and merged things with one another. Supposing she *did* go off into this trance, a kind of hysteria caused by guilt. Supposing Wilberforce was frightened, and stood up, away from her, not knowing what to do. Supposing he was attacked then and carried off. And supposing the young woman, coming out of the trance, began to scream, and was then attacked by Wilberforce's assailant. Could you accept this as an explanation, Adam?"

Dimitry, who had been listening open-mouthed, was surprised by the question and didn't answer immediately. They waited for him, until he gulped, much as he had with Atkinson, before saying:

"*I'm* coming out of a trance, if you ask me! Well—yes, I suppose it does add up. Yes, I think I could believe it."

"Bess?" asked Cellini.

"It's becoming the only feasible explanation to me," Bess said, and then raised her head sharply, and demanded: "Is that what you meant by Wilberforce being 'spirited away'?"

"Yes," answered Cellini. "I think the girl might have been so shocked by her realisation of the enormity of her own offence that she tried to shut it out of her mind, to pretend it hadn't happened—only, on coming back to reality, to find a man with her. He may, for all we know, have tried to rape her; and she would think her lover was not satisfied." Cellini paused, and then asked: "Eh, Scobie?"

"Surely that's not hard to believe," agreed Scobie. "She had shock after hysteria, and if she suddenly convinced herself that she was betraying her friends, family, faith, herself, that she was a scarlet woman—yes, Doctor. It seems feasible to me. I've known men do some pretty queer things after concussion or with shell shock. *Yes*," he repeated with greater emphasis, "it looks as if you've got it. What we had to explain was the time factor."

Bess said: "Yes, I suppose so." Then more briskly: "Yes, it could have happened that way." She looked at Cellini, obviously not yet wholly satisfied, and went on: "But when she talked to me of being possessed by the devil she wasn't hysterical."

"Subdued hysteria?" suggested Scobie.

"She was working up towards an outburst," Bess reported, "but she seemed genuinely frightened. Horrified. That's the thing which I can't get out of my mind. There was a deep sense of shame in her, and the only way she could explain it was that she had been possessed of the devil."

Silence followed the last word and gave it strange emphasis.

Dimitry shifted his position slowly, scuffing his feet. Scobie took out a very white handerchief and blew his nose: the resultant honk was louder than he intended. Only Bess and Cellini continued to stare at each other in silence, as if seeking understanding, perhaps trying to read each other's minds. For the first time, Cellini stood up from the desk and stepped to the window, saying:

"You think she believed this possession by evil, then?"

"Yes," Bess answered. "Yes, I do. That doesn't mean that I believe it."

"No, no, of course not," agreed Cellini. "One doesn't have to believe a hypothesis because someone else does. I think one thing has become apparent to all of us, and that is the very strict training she has received, either from her father, or as a member of the commune. Far from being even remotely irreligious, she is behaving as if she has been brought up in the most extreme fundamentalist way. How else could she so obviously believe that she was possessed of the devil?" Cellini paused before going on: "Such a strength of belief can pass itself on to others— such as to you, Bess. The experience made such

an impression on you that you found yourself
thinking that the man had been spirited away,
whereas if I am right in divining what happened,
then he didn't vanish into thin air, only from her
mind. Physically, he simply walked away. And as
there were other couples in Pucklebury Ring
there is a possibility that he was heard and con-
ceivably seen. But now I am trespassing on your
ground, Inspector! And I have no doubt that
all these possibilities are being explored." He
smiled, but hesitantly, as if more worried than
amused. "Chief Superintendent Hardy mentioned a man who was there last night, a man
named Dee. I believe with an unusual first
name."

"Clipper Dee," confirmed Scobie, and then he
slapped the desk with the palm of his hand.
"Good God—he could have killed Wilberforce!
If the girl's screams began as she came out of this
trance or shock, the time factor has gone hay-
wire. The sooner I talk to Clipper again, the better." His hand went towards the telephone but
he withdrew it. There was a change in the mood,
however, the sense of a family group had broken
up.

Cellini turned his back to the window, and said
quietly:

"There is one important thing we could easily
overlook, you know."

The attention of all three switched to him in-
stantly, and no one asked "What's that?" or

spoke at all, just waited on his words. He
smoothed his moustache again, but this time did
not smile. He had the air of an Old Testament
prophet, and looked very slightly Jewish.

"I think, indeed I hope we know what happened. We have the murderer to find, of course.
But we have another problem, one which is very
acute indeed. If the girl was so easily pushed
over the edge into hysteria, if the fear of being
possessed by the devil was so real, then she must
have been conditioned to this for a long time, a
very long time. And as I see the situation it is as
important to find out who trained her to such
fundamental fervour as to find the man who
killed her lover. For whoever trained her might
have realised that she had betrayed all he had
taught her, and have believed it right to kill."

Dimitry seemed to press against the back of
the chair, he looked so startled. Scobie brushed a
hand over his puckered lips and said heavily:
"Yes." But Cellini paid little attention to either as
he watched Bess. She sat still with her hands
folded in the lap of her dark blue uniform, her
ankles crossed, her eyes turned towards Cellini.
After a few moments she asked in a faraway
voice:

"Could it really be one and the same man, do
you think?"

"The man who conditioned her to fear of being possessed of the devil being also the man
who killed Wilberforce?" Cellini's lips pursed

again, pushing the moustache back. "Yes," he
went on. "Obviously this could be possible.
There are many possibilities, mind you, but this
one certainly must not be overlooked." Then he
added as if to himself: "I do not like the situation. I do not like it at all." But he smiled at Bess
and his tone brightened. "It is almost as if one
can smell the evil spirits who spirited the murderer away, isn't it? Now! A word with you all,
please. Do *not* allow the newspapers to know that
we have discussed this particular aspect. Do *not*
allow talk of the devil to become common. If the
newspapers should seize upon it, our difficulties
at Merryfield could increase very severely indeed. You all understand that, don't you?"

Dimitry promised: "I won't say a word."

"Of course not," muttered Scobie.

"I wonder if I should have put that 'possessed
of the devil' comment in my report," Bess said
uneasily.

"I will tell you one thing," Cellini said, looking
at his most cherubic. "I discussed this with Superintendent Atkinson before you arrived, and
asked him if he took it seriously. I—oh—I am
afraid I told him that I did. He was *most* vehe-
ment in his disagreement. I do advise all of you
not to utter the words 'possessed of the devil' to
your chief. And now, I hope someone can take
me to what is known as the scene of the crime,
where the others should still be working. Unless,
of course, they have already gone on to the

Merryfield Community to talk with the Patriarch about his daughter and about the dead member of his flock."

"Doctor," Bess said, startled. "I have never known you sound bitter before."

"I don't think I have faced such a case as this before," Cellini rejoined.

It was a long time before Scobie broke the silence that followed with a gruff: "I'll take you, sir."

"Thank you," said Cellini. "Thank you, Inspector." Then he added a phrase which made Scobie's heart glow. "I wish it were possible to work always with officers as receptive as you." They went out and down the narrow, rubber-covered stairs into the square hall with its tall doors with high gloss paint, out into the street where only two newspapermen lingered, one of them of course with a camera. A policeman opened the door of Scobie's car, for Cellini. The camera clicked. The reporter, a man with vivid red hair, came up; his face was a mass of freckles, creased to a merriness at eyes and lips.

"Solved it yet, Manny?" he asked.

"Solving the mystery will be a matter for the police, as you well know," said Cellini with mock severity. "And if they are in their usual excellent form I am sure it will not take long." He settled in next to Scobie, who started off with the camera focused on the car. Soon, he turned a corner, then another into the High Street where shoppers passed a medieval barn and two houses with Elizabethan staircases opening on to the paved street. Two sets of traffic lights with swift-passing traffic and three zebra crossings thronged with people were hazards which kept both men quiet. An elderly woman made a lunatic dash to beat one set of lights and Scobie jammed on his brakes, jolting Cellini forward.

"Sorry," he ejaculated. "There's one born every minute."

"Inspector," Cellini said in a tone of mild reproof, "each man in his time is a fool. The man whom I have found a fool less often—much less often—than most is Chief Superintendent Hardy. You may know already, but he is a remarkable man as well as a fine policeman. And *most* understanding. *Most* understanding," repeated Cellini.

7

Halling Forest

JOHN HARDY STOOD, with Atkinson beside him, in the middle of the glen where Wilberforce's body had been found. Among the trees and shrubs, searching the long grass and the trodden grass, pushing aside the ferns with their tight-curled tops like fangs of an invisible dragon preparing to strike, were twenty or more police-men, some from the division and some from Scotland Yard. They were searching for any-thing which might prove a clue to the killer.

The Commander was standing by the spot where Carol Smith had lain. A large man with a mane of curly greying-brown hair surrounding a bald spot; massive shoulders tapering to a small waist and narrow hips, the Commander looked

more like a wrestler, even a film star, than a
world-renowned detective. Beyond him was a
battery of cameras and newspapermen, inter-
spersed among bushes and trees and ferns.

The Commander's name was Bull, almost
unbelievably, John Bull.

He stood up from the spot, where he had in
fact been posing for the Press men, as Hardy
knew well. Bull had always been an extrovert,
something of an exhibitionist, a showman; and
as such he had done a great job of public relations for the Yard.

He joined Hardy and Atkinson, who were now
out of ear-shot of all but one or two of their own
men. The sun shone warm not only here but at a
spot, marked out with stakes and tapes, where
Wilberforce's body had been found. It was a little after one o'clock and Hardy already felt that
he had had a long day. Atkinson dabbed his
sweaty forehead; at the shoulders he and Bull
were about the same size, but Atkinson's body
ballooned into a huge paunch where Bull's fell
away to a tapering slenderness.

"Well, Commander," Atkinson said loudly.
"Halling has one of the finest pubs in England
and one of the finest cooks. Not one of these
new-fangled *chefs* with their tarted-up gourmet-
stuff but a real cook who provides the best tradi-
tional English food. I took the precaution of
reserving a table, as it gets very crowded. Bursts
at the seams some days."

"That sounds very good." Bull had a lowpitched voice; rumour said that once he had started up the ladder of the Metropolitan Police he had studied voice and deportment, and certainly he had a pleasing way of speaking. "But have we time?"

"Time?" exclaimed Atkinson. "We can make time."

"Chief Superintendent," Bull said to Hardy, almost as if they were strangers, "do I understand that the names of the victim and the girl have been withheld from the Press?"

"Yes." Hardy answered. "Until we have had time to talk to the people at Merryfield."

"I must admit, it isn't what I would have done," Atkinson observed. "Treat the Press fairly and it will treat you fairly, that's always been my axiom."

"Why?" Bull asked Hardy.

"Because once it's known where they came from the newspapers and television are going to hit the sky," Hardy replied.

"Because of this community living experiment there, you mean?"

"They've been waiting to have a go for a long time."

"If people behave like oddities they must be prepared to be treated as oddities," Atkinson declared in a resonant whisper.

"What makes you so sensitive about them?" asked Bull.

"*Cellini!*" Atkinson blurted out. "I simply don't think it right that a man outside the Force should be given such privileges. I don't consider it right."

"I'm sure you don't, Reggie," Hardy soothed. "But this is a strange affair—"

"Nothing strange about it. Young couple get up to no good among the bushes. Husband or jealous lover appears. Can understand it perfectly. Can't really say I blame him, this is one of the cases where I have to admit the law to abolish hanging has a point. Fellow has to be caught and punished, of course, but if ever anyone asked for trouble, this Wilberforce did. And the fact that they both came from this den of iniquity called Merryfield—*what* a misnomer!—is no reason why anyone's feelings should be considered. Let the truth be known as soon as possible, I say."

As he finished, Atkinson was breathing very heavily.

Hardy thought: Thank God he's only a few months off retirement, and made sure Bull didn't want to speak before he spoke again in the same placatory tone and manner. He hoped the Press was really out of earshot, and then decided that it didn't greatly matter; the Community would have to be visited very soon and no story the newspapers told would do any real harm now.

"I wanted to be sure we knew as much as we could before going to the Community," he explained. Particularly as Dr. Cellini had already been consulted there."

"Bloody nonsense!" exclaimed Atkinson.

"What is?" asked Bull mildly.

"Talk of the devil!"

"I don't follow," said Bull, understandably.

"If you'd been there you'd know what I mean," said Atkinson in a strangled voice. It was as if he knew that if he didn't control himself he would explode. In between words and phrases he was breathing very hard. "Cellini actually *said* he'd been consulted by the man they call the Patriarch—imagine, in this day and age, the Patriarch!—because he thought the devil was at large in the Community. I wonder he didn't ask the Bishop of Bentfield to go and exorcise the place. And if it isn't bad enough to have a Patriarch frightened of the devil, Cellini said he thought there might be some reason in it. My God! I gave him a piece of my mind, I can tell you, friend of Superintendent Hardy or not."

Atkinson wiped his neck and lips and forehead, his exertions had made him sweat so much; and now his breathing was very heavy indeed: almost gasping. But he did not appear to be aware of it.

"I didn't want to go to the Community with a half-story—" Hardy began.

"You mean *Cellini* persuaded you to stay away," Atkinson rasped.

"Reggie," Hardy said with remarkable patience. "I know Manny upset you and I know you didn't like it when I asked you to keep away from the Community until I'd had a chance to come here, but—"

"You *and* Cellini."

"Yes, of course," Hardy admitted. "I think he can help."

"*I* think that if the murderer was from the Community he's probably a hundred miles away by now!"

"A man who can be identified as missing from the Community will be easy to pick up," Hardy replied. "And in any case I don't agree with you. Once he left the Community he would be immediately suspect. While he stays there he's less likely to attract our attention. But the point is, sir, I do respect Manny's opinion and he did ask for this opportunity." Defensively, he went on: "Nothing else has been delayed."

"*I* saw to that," growled Atkinson.

Hardy stayed silent, watching the distant trees, aware of the searching men making their methodical way through Pucklebury Ring; not a single useful find had been made that morning. He deliberately kept his gaze away from Bull, not sure what the other's reaction would be. Just what had got under Atkinson's skin so much he didn't know; it could be a simple matter of pride or injured vanity. The first indication that things had gone wrong was when the Halling superin-

tendent had exploded in his office, just before
Scobie had brought the other two officers in.

"Reggie," Bull said unexpectedly, "the more I
think of that pub the more I like it. And I'd like
you to fill me in over the local situation. John, I
want you to go to this Community and take Dr.
Cellini with you. Make it clear to the—*what* do
you call the leader?"

"The Patriarch," Atkinson said with disgust.

"This so-called Patriarch that although he had
consulted Dr. Cellini first, Dr. Cellini will now
have to co-operate with the police as well. I'm
sure Cellini understands that very well," he went
on. "Then we'll have a conference at Reggie's office later this afternoon—four-thirty, say—and
decide on the right course of action. Well,
Reggie, let's go and see if that food is all you say
it is!"

Gratification overcoming his exasperation and
disapproval, Atkinson led the Commander towards the parked cars. Hardy watched them
drive off and then spoke to the Divisional Superintendent in charge of the search. About fifty or
sixty things had been found, from a wristwatch
to a penknife, eleven lipsticks or other make-up
aids, several keys, handkerchiefs, one wallet with
money inside and everything to identify the
owner, a lot of odd silver coins, two pairs of
stockings and a set of panty-hose.

Each "find" had been placed in a plastic envel-

ope or bag, sealed with a twist of covered wire
and tagged; the exact location was entered, the
finder, a brief description of the article. But all
of these things had been lying in the Ring for
several days. Two packets of cigarettes looked
new enough to have been left at the spot last
night, but nothing else did.

"We'll go through it carefully at the station,"
the C.I.D. man in charge assured Hardy. "But I
doubt if anything here will be any use to us."

"Keep trying," Hardy urged, and added:
"Couldn't be a neater job."

"Thank you, sir."

Hardy heard a car approaching, looked round
and saw Detective Inspector Scobie with Cellini
by his side. Cellini was looking about with his
customary attention; for a man in his late sixties
he had remarkable vitality and alertness, and he
missed little. More important, whenever he saw
something he put a mental tag on it, and also
formed a quick and usually correct opinion of its
significance. Hardy went across to them as a man
from the search party sprang forward to open
the door.

"You are really alone," Cellini exclaimed, in
disbelief.

"The others have gone off to have lunch,"
Hardy rejoined, "and we're going to miss ours or
just have a snack before we go to the Community. I don't want to lose any more time,
though."

"I'm not hungry," Cellini announced promptly.

"I had a late breakfast and a coffee snack." volunteered Scobie.

"I can manage," said Hardy. "Let's go."

"What about the Press?" asked Scobie.

"They won't be in the way yet," Hardy said. "The main entrance of the Community is being watched, isn't it?"

"Yes, sir. And it's the only entrance for vehicles, although there are one or two footpaths."

"Just tell your chaps on duty at the entrance that no one's to come in," said Hardy. "Can you do shorthand?"

"Yes, sir."

"Then we three will be enough," Hardy declared. "And on the way, Manny, you'd better tell us what you can of this man who calls himself the Patriarch, and what he's doing here—or trying to do."

"What he is trying to do," answered Cellini after a remarkably short pause, "is to create a new and happier way of living. A way which will make a new world." He allowed time for that to sink in, and then went on: "What he is doing is a different matter—as indeed what others are doing in the Community is a different matter. There are in all fifty couples, and forty-seven children. The Community is virtually self-supporting. Most of the men do a job—many are professional men but some are skilled workers such as engineers. Each family contributes in cash and kind to the needs of the whole, and the amount placed in the pool is shared equally. Except for their daily needs outside the Community, going to and from work, for instance, and eating—no one has more than anyone else. Private possessions are limited to a very few personal belongings. No one has a bank account or savings, stocks or shares, property or furniture, outside the Community. There are schools of a kind, actually a system of tutoring by qualified teachers. I can tell you that the Halling Educational Authority accepts the system up to the age of eleven when the older children have to go to comprehensive or grammar schools—or public schools. There are two private schools which run on similar lines to the Community, so most of the children go there."

Cellini paused after this torrent of words, and looked at the others intently; obviously to find out how much they had taken in. Hardy had missed some details but was mainly concerned with the clear proof that Cellini knew a great deal about the Community, and was well disposed towards it. He made no comment, but Scobie said:

"I already knew something of this, sir."

"Do you know of anything against the Community?"

"No," answered Scobie, speaking slowly and thoughtfully. "One or two of the more narrow-minded church—I should say religious—groups, have objected on moral grounds, accusing the Community of practicing free love. And a few of the more hearty types talk about it being a wife-swapping centre. But so far as we are concerned, I mean the police, sir, there has been absolutely nothing wrong. We've never had complaints about noise or riotous living, even from the Russell Estate, which is fairly near and an expensive and exclusive residential one." He thought of Dimitry and the altercation with his wife. "When they first came here, it must be fifteen years ago now, the Community was in the heart of the country, of course, and they selected the spot because they could grow most of the fruit and vegetables they need. They fatten some cattle for Community consumption, too."

"Most gratifying to know that you have studied the Community with such interest and accuracy," Cellini said. "John, there isn't much more to say. There are many details, of course. They have their own swimming pool and recreation area, they have their own library, cinema, theatre group. They have visits from mobile libraries, travelling art exhibitions and cultural exhibitions of all kinds. They make up parties to go to various places outside Halling—theatres, occasionally museums and churches. They are in fact a community within a community and I believe that until a few months ago, they had a fair chance of success. Then—I don't know whether you ever heard of this, Inspector—a new and disruptive element entered the Community. Someone among them did not want the experiment to succeed. Fear stalked, where for a long time there had been freedom from fear. And it looks to me as if what happened last night is an extension of what has been happening within the Community. And among those who live there some are already beginning to ask if this could be the work of the devil."

"And they take this literally? asked Hardy, with fascinated if incredulous interest.

"That is one of the things we are surely going to find out," Cellini said.

As he spoke, they came within sight of the entrance to Merryfield, where four policemen were on duty. One police car was tucked beneath the hedge, while several newspapermen and cameramen stood about, near the post marked *Bus Stop*. None of the men attempted to slow down Scobie's car as he turned into the gravel drive.

8

The Patriarch

HIGH LAUREL AND rhododendron hedges rose
on either side, so that they could see nothing except the dusty gravel road ahead. There was so
much dust that the hedges were coated with a
layer of pale brown. The surface was good, as if
it were not used a great deal. After half-a-mile
the hedge flattened and they appeared suddenly
to have come into a small farm, or market garden. Six or seven women and two men were
working at the crops which looked young and
healthy. Dotted about the cultivated land were
small patches of fruit trees, perhaps twenty or
thirty in each "orchard." On one side were some
long greenhouses, on which the sun glinted. The
road wound on past beds of outdoor tomatoes,

already showing signs of ripening. A large cage
for soft fruit was on the other side of the road
from the greenhouses.

They turned a corner, beyond which was a
copse of beech; and here, obviously, was the
heart of the Community.

It was not, in a way, unlike Pucklebury Ring.

The trees, in full leaf, were grouped against
the brow of a hill. Nestled against them, and
even amongst them, were cottages, all of wood,
all rather like Swiss chalets, although some were
single storey buildings. All had tile or shingle
roofs. Each had a small patch of garden, and
many of these were vivid with bright flowers.
Two women in ankle-length dresses were standing at the doorway of one house, looking towards the oncoming car, but neither moved towards it.

One thing was immediately apparent: no
fences or hedges divided the houses.

On one side, across what could be called a village green, were larger buildings, all attractively
designed: these, obviously, were the communal
centres; indeed there was an appetising smell
particularly penetrating when Scobie wound
down a window. Between the small houses and
the larger buildings, and half-way up the slope
leading to the trees, was a house larger than any
of the others. It was also of wood, painted white,
and it had a huge window which overlooked all
the rest of the Community.

"That is the Patriarch's home," Cellini announced.

"So it *isn't* exactly the same for everyone," Scobie remarked.

"He has his home in the administration building," Cellini replied.

"I see, sir."

"How often have you been here?" asked Hardy.

"On three occasions," answered Cellini. "Three in all."

"So you know the Patriarch well?"

"I doubt if it would be possible to know him really well," replied Cellini. "But I am familiar with some of his thinking."

"Is he married?" asked Hardy.

"He lives here alone," said Cellini.

"Just with his daughter."

"No," Cellini answered. "Carol lives with a group of unwedded girls—there are two houses for young people, one for each sex. As Joshua Smith will no doubt tell you," Cellini went on, "one of the foundations of the Community is the belief that after puberty the children do not belong exclusively to the parents but to the Community. The parents continue to look after them some of the time but the responsibility is shared."

"Rather like the Jewish kibbutz," suggested Scobie.

Cellini gave him a long, penetrating look, and then said: "Yes, in some ways. Merryfield is not an original idea although it has many novel aspects." He stopped, pausing now at the house. "Usually someone comes out to welcome visitors," he went on. "John, who is to break the news to Smith?"

"And Wilberforce's wife," Scobie added under his breath.

"I would like you to," said Hardy. "I—hallo! The door's opening."

The door he meant was one by the long window, and at one end of the front of the house. On either side were sweeping lawns, beautifully kept; in the near-distance a vegetable garden and some fruit trees could be seen.

A man appeared, and no one was likely to doubt that this was the Patriarch.

He was not large, although he was broad and solid-looking. He wore a pale tunic with a sash at the waist, the skirt of which fell half-way to his knees, and a pair of narrow trousers of a darker shade of grey. He moved with long and powerful-seeming strides. All of these things were striking, but the most striking one of all was his face. The spade-shaped beard, black shot with white, and the plentiful dark hair, somehow threw his fine eyes and forehead and the delicacy of his features into relief. He looked more as if he were carved out of alabaster than made of flesh and blood. He might be anywhere between forty and fifty, but was probably nearer fifty; as the others got out of the car they could see the lines round his eyes and lips, even one or two already creasing his cheeks. His eyes were pale grey and, when they caught the light, had a look of polished steel.

He smiled, just enough to show his lips, and said: "I am glad to see you, Dr. Cellini. I see you have brought friends with you." He looked at Scobie with greater interest than at Hardy, as if at someone who was familiar.

"An old friend and a new one," Cellini said.

"They are very welcome."

"They do not come with welcome news," Cellini replied. "John Hardy here is also Chief Detective Superintendent Hardy of New Scotland Yard, and Detective Inspector Scobie is from the Halling divisional police station."

"Ah!" exclaimed Joshua Smith. "That is where I have seen you, Mr. Scobie. I had once to call at the police station and you were there." He shook hands with each man. "What brings you here with the police, Dr. Cellini?"

"Unhappy news," Cellini replied.

"Not, I trust, to do with the work you have undertaken for me."

At first the Patriarch's voice had appeared to be rather high-pitched but it had a firm and attractive timbre. He was obviously native English; there was even something about his appearance which put that beyond doubt. He had a natural ease of manner, and obviously great self-confidence, but there was anxiety in his expression as he studied Cellini.

"I think it may be to do only with this place," Cellini said, "and you were not told earlier because I was anxious to be present. I hope you will forgive me for causing the delay."

"It will be acutely distressing if it is about Merryfield," replied Smith, and spared a glance for Hardy. "Have you told your friends about my overall problem?"

"In general, yes. In detail, no. But it may become necessary to tell them in the greatest detail," Cellini went on. "That was why I wanted to come with them, to help explain."

"You mean, to break bad news gently," remarked Smith with a wry smile. He turned and led the way towards the house, a pace ahead of Cellini who was several paces ahead of the others. It would be easy to believe that it looked as if he wanted to hide his face from them. But his tread was firm and there was no hint of faltering. He was on the path which led across the grass towards the front door when at last he glanced over his shoulder.

"Do you need food, Dr. Cellini?"

"All of us would find a little food welcome," Cellini answered promptly.

"I will be happy if you will join me," said Joshua Smith. "I have been delayed this morning and have not yet had a midday meal." He opened the door and led them into a large room, the one with the panoramic window. The wooden floor, highly polished, was dotted with handmade woollen rugs. The furniture, all of which looked comfortable, was of wood frame-work, upholstered with a loose weave fabric, like a coarse canvas. The blending of pastel colours, from pinks and browns, greens and blues, yellows and greys, was made more attractive by the two snow-white and the two ebony-black couches, against the longer walls. There were two long tables and several smaller ones, each made of wood polished on the top, but rough-hewn at the sides. On the walls were several pictures; of people, of landscapes, of farmhouses and of cattle. All of these were competently executed, though none was brilliant. At one end of the room was a dining-table with chairs in the same simple style, and opposite this, a door stood ajar. Smith went straight to the door, opened it wide, and called:

"Elizabeth!"

A woman answered in a pleasant voice: "Yes, Joshua."

"Can you prepare a table for four?"

"Of course," the woman called, from the door-way. She smiled and went on: "It is nice to see you again, Dr. Cellini."

"A very great pleasure to me," Cellini said, extravagantly. It was at such moments that his European origins came out, with a touch almost of flamboyance which surprised those who knew him as more English than the English.

Smith did not introduce the two men to her, obviously not wishing her to know, yet, that they were policemen.

Hardy, mildly surprised by the naturalness of both man and woman, watched Smith take a flagon of beer or cider from a cupboard in a corner and then produce four tall, frosted glasses, of unusual shape and make; they looked like hollowed out logs of transparent wood.

It was cider: sharp and full of flavour. Scobie appeared to smack his lips.

"We make our own cider from our own orchards," Smith announced, drinking with relish. He held the glass chest-high and went on with a slight change of voice and a noticeable tensing of his expression.

"What is your news, Emmanuel?"

"Do you know that Carol has not been home all night," asked Cellini.

"Yes," Smith answered.

"Has it worried you?"

"She has her own life and leads it as she wishes," Smith replied. "I have of course been worried about her at times but then—" he shrugged slightly—"she has the benefit of the advice of many others. One of the great causes of worry and anxiety is the knowledge that one has failed in one's responsibilities to one's children. Here, as you know well, we share that re-

sponsibility and we train the young to accept responsibility for themselves." He raised his arms
and dropped them to his sides. "Yet I am
worried, as I would be for any young person in
the Community, and yes—more because she is
my own." He squared his shoulders and shifted
his gaze to Hardy. "What has happened to her?"
He held his breath for a moment before de-
manding: "Is she dead?"

"No," Hardy replied. "We know she was attacked, however, and involved in much
violence."

For a moment Smith closed his eyes, but soon
he opened them and asked in a husky voice: "Is
she well?"

"She is badly shocked and now under sedation
but apart from the psychological damage of the
attack, she is not hurt."

"That at least is a relief," Smith said. "And psychological injury, if known, can be repaired. May
I ask a question?"

"As many as you like," said Hardy.

"Do you know why she was attacked?"

"We are not sure, but have some reason to
think it was partly because she had taken a
lover," Hardy replied.

"For a young girl to take a lover would hardly
be unusual," Smith said. "Or—" Behind his
beard and moustache he smiled wryly: his lips
were pale and seemed very moist. "Or even by
the standards both here and in most of the out-

side world, immoral. But you have not really answered my question. Why should she be attacked
for such a reason?"

"That would depend on the identity of her
lover," Cellini remarked very gently. "Here in
the Community it would be significant. Joshua,
do you know that Lionel Wilberforce is
missing?"

Smith's face seemed to lock itself into a set expression; his jaw thrust forward, his eyes more
narrowed than since they had been here. He
stood up very slowly and walked to the window,
surveying the sweeping lawns, the beech and
birch and oak trees, the small houses merging so
beautifully. The two women who had been talking were now laughing, their heads thrown back.
They were about to part, the one to walk away
from a house, the other to go into it. Outside,
there was peace.

Joshua Smith turned, and on his face was the
tension of anguish.

"Was the man concerned Lionel?" he demanded.

"Yes," Cellini told him.

"And *he* went with Carol?"

"Yes."

"No woman is safe from him," Smith stated in
a strangled voice. "No one in the Community
can be trusted with him. He is known to have seduced and to have slept with at least four of the
married women here, and suspected of seducing

two of the younger women from their shared home. Carol is not the first; and the fact that he has seduced my daughter makes his behaviour neither better nor worse." Smith paused, his jaw working visibly beneath the beard. When he spoke again it was as if speech were difficult: "He must go. There is no other way to cope."

"Go where?" demanded Hardy.

"Away from here," Smith answered, coming towards them. The cadence of his voice changed and he used his hands to emphasise his words, more in the manner of an orator than that of a man in discourse with a small group of people. "He, and his wife if she wishes, must be banished. I have known for some months that there was evil stalking this place. Evil and fear and jealousy and hatred, the emotions which I created this community to exorcise from all our members. Lionel Wilberforce has brought them back. In his lust, in his failure to respect the rights and the privileges of other members, in his profligate behaviour, he has forfeited all his own rights and privileges. He *must* be banished." Now the man's hands were raised in front of his chest, palms downwards yet sloping slightly. And the fingers curled. There was great strength in those hands, so much could be seen from the way he held them; they clutched as if at some invisible thing between them, squeezing the air as if it were a human throat. "I shall call a meeting tonight and announce to all the members that only for the

second time since we were founded a man must
be compelled to go."

Smith stopped.

His voice had dropped to a growling note; his
hands still clenched the air. Sweat on his forehead began to roll into his eyes. He appeared to
be a man in torment. He stared, not at them but
above their heads, as if at some invisible sign
high on the wall. The silence that followed
seemed absolute, without even a whisper of
breathing. The three men in front of Smith were
all affected, and Scobie stared before him as if he
were mesmerised.

Then, Emmanuel Cellini spoke.

His voice, always gentle, came so softly that at
first it was hardly sound at all, and no one took
any notice. But it grew and filled the room, its
echoes spreading. There was compassion in the
voice itself, compassion in the words, in his eyes.

"Joshua, there is even worse news, I fear. I am
the saddest of men to have to bring it to you." He
paused, but so far Smith did not appear to have
heard him. He was still staring at the spot above
their heads. Scobie followed his glance, but he
could see nothing except the plain wood. "You
will not need to banish Lionel," Cellini went on:
"He is dead."

The word seemed to echo: "Dead—ead—
ead." Lingering, it seemed to reach Joshua
Smith at last. His trance-like stance changed. He

looked at Cellini with a startled manner, then took a step forward.

"*Dead*? Did he die of his own hand, in shame?"

"No," answered Cellini, and because his voice was so gentle and his manner, too, the words took on a cruel harshness; each one a barb carrying its own pain. "He was murdered. Strangled. The police are with me because they must find out if there is a murderer in the Community. And they need your help, Joshua: they need your help very much."

Joshua, fully understanding now, his expression touched with horror, took a step towards them. And from the inside door there was a gasp followed by a crash as crockery fell from the hands of the woman who must have been close to the partly open door.

9

Murderer in the Midst

ONLY SMITH AND Cellini failed to look towards the door. They stood, as protagonists, while the clattering and the breaking slackened and stopped. Scobie, nearest the door, turned to see the woman leaning against the door jamb, face in her hands, the broken corckery about her feet. Hardy had a glimpse of this, too, but was so intent on Smith that he spared only a glance. The horror slowly faded from Smith's face; it was as if he had absorbed the shock of the news quickly, and it had brought him out of the near-trance of his oration. Perhaps to conceal his expression, perhaps out of natural reaction, he moved towards the woman, opened the door wider and put his arms round her shoulders.

She was not crying, but shaking as if from shock.
Smith led her into the room, not out of it, and
stood by the great window, while she buried her
face against his shoulder; her hands covered her
gold-coloured hair.

Scobie moved across and began to pick up the
broken pieces, placing small fragments onto a
plate that had only a chip out of it. The aroma of
cooking came clearly, enticingly. The little
clinking noises made the only sound until Joshua
Smith said quietly:

"There is no need for this distress, Elizabeth.
You are upsetting yourself too much." After a
pause he went on: "Look at me."

She did not move her head for a while but at
last took her hands away and peered into his
face. Her eyes were tear-damp but no tears were
on her cheeks. She had on no lipstick and, although very pale her complexion was unusually
good.

She seemed oblivious of everyone else in the
room.

"I am sorry," she said in an unsteady voice. "I
shall be all right now."

"I'm sure you will be," Smith said. "Fend for
us, please."

"Elizabeth," interpolated Cellini, in that most
gentle voice, "why were you so shocked?" When
she did not answer at once he moved towards
her, hands stretched out appealingly, and now
she had to look at him; and so did Smith, who

was frowning as if puzzled and surprised. "These gentlemen are police officers," Cellini went on. "Chief Superindendent Hardy is from Scotland Yard. Detective Inspector Scobie from Halling police station. They have to find a murderer. As I told Joshua, they need his help. They need your help, too, and the way everyone can help most is by telling the truth." He paused long enough for that to sink in, before adding: "If I were either of them I would think it strange that you were so shocked—shocked out of self-control. Their task is to gather and assess the facts. They cannot read your mind and they do not know you as well as I have come to in the short time we have known each other. I am sure there must be a very good and innocent reason for your reaction, but they don't know any such thing."

The woman glanced away from them and looked at Smith, who was still watching Cellini closely. But he was smiling, faintly, and no longer looked puzzled or surprised.

"Elizabeth," he said. "I am not only sure that Dr. Cellini is a friend but also very wise. When you have served lunch I want you to go to the homes and tell all our people that they must give the police all the information and assistance they can. And before serving lunch please tell us all why you were so badly shaken."

She looked at him with tear-dimmed bright eyes. She was a striking woman with a broad forehead and vivid blue eyes, the fullness of her figure concealed by a toga-like dress of pale blue. Her hesitation might have been due to uncertainty or defiance. Her voice was steady and her manner forthright as she went on:

"Isn't the fact of murder enough?"

"Not if it is less than the whole truth," answered Smith.

"One of our members is murdered, and I am supposed not to be shocked?"

"Not to be so shocked," Cellini put in quietly.

"But I *was* so shocked."

"Simply because of what you heard?" asked Smith.

"Yes," Elizabeth answered. "At least—" she hesitated, and put a hand against her forehead. "That was a bombshell, Joshua. I have been so worried and concerned about the changes here. The fear—the *failure*," she went on challengingly. "Everything you worked and planned for is breaking about our ears."

"Elizabeth—" Smith raised his hand and raised his voice.

"Joshua," she said, and there was now no doubt of her mood of defiance. "You ask me to tell the truth. Am I to conceal part of it?"

He began: "The truth so far as your reaction to —" and then broke off; this was the first sign of weakness in the man. Again he stepped to the window and looked out at the sylvan scene; and again he turned and stared at the wall above their heads. It seemed a long time before he said: "No, you are quite right. Say whatever is in your mind. I do not agree with you that there is failure and collapse. Danger, perhaps, but we can avert the consequences if we face the situation boldly."

"Joshua," she said into the lull after he had finished, "I care for the Community as much as you. Many of us do. We have been distressed and frightened by what has happened. Fear has been in everyone, that our efforts would be wasted, that we should break up in failure. We do not all have your strength and your faith. You may be able to withstand failure but I cannot. I have been afraid of what would happen to me if the Community collapsed. For a while you would not even admit there was any danger and when you asked Dr. Cellini for help most of us were greatly relieved. We were given new hope. Now, one of our number has been murdered after seducing not one but six or seven women and girls here. So, vengeance has been done. And the police must question everyone closely. The newspapers will probe as deeply as they can. Our privacy, our right to lead our own lives in the way we think best, will be taken from us because an evil man was in our midst, and another may well be among us—he who killed in vengeance and hatred because—" she closed her eyes and stretched out a hand as if pleadingly, but suddenly she was wide-eyed again; and the blue in them seemed to burn. "Because you were not able to deal with the situation, Joshua. I hate to say this, but it was because you failed.

"Is that not enough to make me collapse in despair?"

The woman Elizabeth had retired to the back of the house.

The Patriarch, Joshua Smith, had followed her, and the door was closed.

Cellini stood looking out of the window, his hands clasped lightly in front of him. The sunlight had shifted so that it now struck a corner of the window, slashing across the grass and trees. Hardy was sitting back in one of the easy chairs. Scobie was picking up a few small pieces of china which had fallen inside the room. Hardy leaned back against the padded top of his chair and said:

"Well, Manny?"

"Who has failed, I wonder?" Cellini asked reflectively.

"If you are beginning to blame yourself because you didn't come here and work a miracle, stop the nonsense at once," urged Hardy. "You were probably the only man who could even begin to help them. If the experiment proves a failure it's a failure because of some inherent quality in it."

Cellini frowned but did not look at him.

"I do not want the Community to be a failure," he declared.

"You are the last man in the world to indulge in wishful thinking."

"And the last man in the world to admit that this *is* a failure," Cellini retorted more briskly. "Now, John, what is your assessment of the situation? Eh? Do you think Elizabeth told the truth? Or do you think the news of Wilberforce's death had some personal significance for her?"

"If I had to bet I would say it had some personal significance," Hardy admitted.

"Which the Patriarch probably knew about," Scobie said straightening up.

"And tried to head off," agreed Hardy. "I don't know what the standards are here, Manny, but I think we had a great deal of evasiveness. I once had an impression that we were going to deal with simple, straightforward people, but these folk appear to be as complicated as anyone outside."

"Considerably more complicated," admitted Cellini. "They haven't created their world of truth, honesty and forgiveness towards human fraility in others, they have simply tried to create it, and in the trying created new problems. I agree with you both. Joshua and Elizabeth both know something they haven't told us."

"Yes," said Hardy, and sent a humorous glance at Scobie. "The more you work with Dr.

Cellini the more you will realise that he has these great flashes of insight! Let me tell you something I shouldn't have to, Manny."

"I shall listen humbly," Cellini said.

"We must really get a move on! Talk to the dead man's wife, bring in a team of men to ask questions, have men here when the workers come back to the Community tonight. I've used kid gloves because I wanted to give you every chance of getting results without turning this into a kind of witch hunt, but I can't wait much longer." He shot Scobie another glance and went on: "In strictest confidence, the Commander took Superintendent Atkinson to lunch so as to give me a free run here for an hour or two. We simply aren't making enough progress, and we have to make up for lost time."

Cellini brushed his moustache gently and thoughtfully, nodded, and then turned with surprising quickness when the door opened and Joshua Smith came in carrying a large tureen. Elizabeth followed with a tray of on which were plates, knives, forks, a crusty loaf of home-made bread, and a crock of butter.

"You are quite right," Smith said. "There must be no further loss of time, no undue studying of other people's feelings, whether they be mine or anyone else's. Elizabeth has given me what I have sadly lacked—a sense of urgency. And that has made me realise that the one hope of saving the Community is to find the murderer quickly.

We shall do everything—*everything* we can to help." He sat down, removed the lid of the tureen, and as the aroma came out with the steam, began to ladle "But I don't think you will detect so well on an empty stomach, will you?"

"Thank you," Hardy said. "Inspector, will you go to your car and call in some of the murder team to work here. Have them arrive in not less than half-an-hour, ready to start."

"Right, sir." Scobie jumped up. He was gone for only two or three minutes, before coming back to report that the arrangements had been made. He met Hardy carrying in a dish of beef stew with dumplings and vegetables piled high. "I'm glad you heard me say we'd have to get cracking, Mr. Smith. And I'm glad you know the newspapers will come crashing down once they know what there is to know. Do you have a P.R.O.?"

"Public relations officer," Smith explained to Elizabeth.

"I know what a P.R.O. is," she replied in near exasperation.

"I am the nearest to one on Merryfield." Smith's spirits had changed quite remarkably. "Why do you ask?"

"The simplest way to keep the Press from pushing too hard is to tell them as much as possible."

"Why don't I invite them here and make a statement," suggested Smith.

"A good idea," approved Hardy. Then he took his first mouthful. "My! That's hot. And good! Your own cooking, Mrs.—" He broke off.

"I am known as Elizabeth," the woman responded smiling. Some kind of load appeared to have been lifted off her mind, too. "All the food here is communally prepared and dishes like this are partly cooked in the main kitchen; those of us who prefer to eat at home fetch what we need and finish the cooking here. I prefer to make my own dumplings!"

"I'm very glad you do."

"Should we set a time for the Press conference?" Scobie suggested, after a moment's pause.

"Shall we say four o'clock," replied Hardy. "If that's all right with you, Mr. Smith?"

"Perfectly," Smith assured him. "What do you need to do before then?"

"First, talk to Lionel Wilberforce's wife," Hardy answered. "Then, check movements in the Community last night as far as we can, to find out if Carol was followed. Whether she went off with Wilberforce or had a rendezvous somewhere else, whether Wilberforce was followed," he explained. He was eating between sentences, proving himself the trencherman of his reputation. "Manny, have you a written record of the statements Mr. Smith has made to you about the problems he has had here?"

"Yes."

"I'd like them, please. I'll have copies taken, and return the originals." He paused to eat but was soon asking more questions. "Mr. Smith, *how* many women has Wilberforce seduced?"

"Seven, to my knowledge," Smith answered.

"How many of these were married?"

"Four lived with their chosen men," Smith said. "In such cases the 'wife' adds the 'husband's' name to hers although this custom is not always followed. On my records Mary is Mary Lee-Wilberforce."

"I see. They weren't actually married by law?"

"Two couples were," replied Smith. "And there were two young women who have been married in the outside world but came here on their own, as well as one young woman, in her late teens, the daughter of one of our oldest couples. It was this child who, questioned because she disappeared from time to time without explanation, first told us that Wilberforce was a seducer, and I, with others, then enquired and found out about the rest."

Hardy finished his stew and with an expression both hopeful and wistful, placed his knife and fork together neatly, and then asked:

"Are there any written rules for the Community, Mr. Smith?"

"There is a code, yes. Will you have more stew?"

"Er—I really shouldn't. Does this written code lay down conditions of membership?" asked Hardy.

"Yes," answered Smith, quietly. "Members have to accept certain codes or standards of behaviour. They do not have to be married in the conventional sense although if they are there is no objection. If a couple shares a home they are considered to be married. They undertake to respect the privacy and the rights of other families, and—but I can provide you with a copy. I do assure you it is very simple and brief."

"Thank you. I—"

"*Do* have a little more," urged Smith. "Ah—I see *you* will, Inspector." He ladled more stew on to each plate but did not attempt to press Cellini to have more although his plate was nearly empty.

"Each of the husbands might have an emotional reason for murdering Wilberforce, then," Hardy said. "Thank you —these dumplings are quite the best I've ever tasted."

"Thank you," Elizabeth gravely smiled.

"An emotional motive, yes," agreed Smith.

"And would the unmarried women and the girl he seduced have boy-friends?"

"They might well have," agreed Smith.

"I gathered from something you said earlier that premarital sex isn't exactly frowned on here." Hardy finished and then placed a piece of gravy-coloured dumpling into his mouth.

"It is not," agreed Smith. "One of our tenets is that premarital sexual intercourse is natural and inescapable, not wrong, and should not be condemned and certainly not banned without doing grave psychological harm. Moreover the consequence of condemning it creates furtiveness and deceit and gives to the completely natural act a smear of guilt, thus creating false values over which other false and hypocritical values are built. So the matter is left entirely to the individuals concerned."

Hardy finished what he was eating, and uttered one word: "Children?"

"In that respect we have an entirely different attitude from the world's conventional one," said Smith, matter-of-factly. Not once since he had come back from the kitchen with Elizabeth had he shown any anxiety or tension; whatever had eased his mind was having a lasting effect. "We do *not* believe in oral birth control. We believe that this disturbs the metabolism of the woman seriously and could affect children born after use of the method. We accept mechanical means, such as condoms and Dutch caps; these are matters for the individual. If children are born as a result of love-making and not within a family, or by a couple who do not wish to live together, these children are cared for by the Community. The mother will feel no sense of shame. She will spend much time with her own child in the first year or two, especially as most of the babies born

here are breast-fed until they are at least nine
months old. After that the mothers simply carry
out their share of communal baby and child-
care. The children of the Community, Superintendent, belong not wholly to individuals but
largely to the Community. In this way, if the af-
fections, and so the relationship, between the
parents change, the child does not suffer. In fact
when the code is followed no one suffers; good,
never harm, is done. I do not pretend," Smith
went on, his voice quietening gradually, "that
this is a wholly novel experiment. Something like
it was the way of life in many Pacific islands before what we now call civilisation overtook them.
Experiments have been tried in many parts of
America and many parts of Europe, some of the
most progressive here in England. What I have
done is to study all the experiments and distilled
the best from each, as far as seemed to me practicable, and so tried to establish a model community on which much of the future of society
could be based.

"I still believe that can be done here," Smith
went on very quietly. "Provided you are quick to
find the killer."

10

"Wife" and Mother

FIVE MINUTES AFTER they finished the meal, with
ample fresh fruit and tasty home-made cheese,
came the first of the police cars. From then on,
the high-pressure investigation, until then concentrated on Pucklebury Ring, was switched to
Merryfield. Twenty police officers, briefed before they had left Halling Divisional Headquarters, began to question the men and women in
the Community about what they had seen the
previous night. A few facts were quickly
established.

Carol Smith had left the camp fire, built at the
edge of an amphitheatre, where they had been
singing and playing guitar and banjo music, at
half-past nine.

Lionel Wilberforce had left for his home and his "wife" about a quarter of an hour later: but his "wife" had not seen him.

The singing and playing group had broken up at half-past ten, always the latest time for music. They played and sang in a man-made amphitheatre with a half-circle of seats, more like steps, dug out of the side of a shallow hill. The amphitheatre, which served as outdoor theatre and lecture hall, faced south, and little noise travelled back to the Community houses; still less to Pucklebury Ring except when the wind was from the south, as it had been the previous night.

All the members whose movements could not be traced completely had been at the amphitheatre at some time during the evening. Only by questioning everyone would it be possible to find out who had left early. Two of the suspects worked in the gardens, one a nursery man who specialised in glasshouse work, one who tended the fruit and staple foods.

All the members were aware of the growing tension in the Community.

Everyone now knew that a crisis had come upon them.

As the men, and those of the younger women who preferred careers outside the Community to domestic and agricultural work inside, returned from London or its suburbs and satellite towns, they found the police waiting.

The Press, given a straightforward statement

of the identity of the murder victim and told that
it was possible that the murderer lived at or visited Merryfield, kept a watchful and inquisitive
survey, but did not push their questions too
hard.

Scobie shared the supervision of the search
with Chief Inspector Robson, a short, stocky, tac-
iturn man who simply got on with his job.

Atkinson, back with Commander Bull when
the investigation had got well under way, appeared to be satisfied and, after a twenty-minute
visit to the Community and a brief talk with
Joshua Smith, went back to his headquarters. He
seemed under the weather, possibly because he
had wined and dined too freely. Bull went with
him, without asking any specific questions but
saying to Hardy just before he left:

"Call me tonight, sometime before eleven
o'clock, John."

"I'll be glad to," Hardy said.

"Don't let Manny have his head too much."

"You needn't worry at all," Hardy assured
him.

"I hope you're right," Bull said. "And don't go
straying into any of these women's arms," he
urged. "They all look pretty bedworthy to me."

"I prefer not to be strangled," Hardy retorted
drily.

Bull joined Atkinson, smiling broadly, and
Hardy watched their car drive off, then stood
and surveyed the scene. It was remarkable that a

few men could make such a difference. There were dozens of people about, as well as some young children who played in earnest concentration or in high spirits at a dozen games, supervised by two young women, one of whom was Mary Lee-Wilberforce. Hardy watched as she carried out her task with simple effectiveness and even temper.

Hardy and Cellini had broken the news to her soon after lunch. Then, obviously shocked, she had run to her children: hers and Wilberforce's. . .

Hardy had decided that she need not identify the body; soon Joshua Smith would go and do this.

All the children seemed happy, but their high spirits had a curiously dampening effect on Hardy. He heard footsteps approaching and glanced round to see Cellini, who had come from the Patriarch's home. They stood together for a few moments before Hardy said:

"It all looks so peaceful on the surface. I almost hate to break it up, but I ought to talk to Mary Wilberforce."

"She will get someone to replace her for the time being," Cellini assured him, and asked with his cutomary directness: "May I come with you?"

"I don't see why not," Hardy conceded. "I was glad of you last time."

He remembered so vividly the first interview with Mary Wilberforce; remembered being

shocked because she looked so young and innocent. Like all the women when inside the Community grounds she wore a kind of toga. Shorter
than Elizabeth's, it ended just above the knees.
She had attractive, if sturdy legs; in fact, despite
her youthfulness, she was a sturdy woman. It
was the freshness of her face, the directness of
her grey eyes, the simplicity of her hair style,
drawn back from the cheeks, that was so appeal-
ing. She had the same kind of flawless complexion as Elizabeth. The toga was drawn fairly high
at the neck, where the fold crossed, but there
was a hint of bosom, a kind of simple
provocativeness.

She had not known her husband was dead.

In a way, Hardy resented the fact that it had
devolved on him to tell her. He did not quite
know how or why except, of course, that Manny
Cellini had really inveigled him into this whole
business. Meek and mild little Manny with a
mind like Machiavelli! There had been some de-
bate as to whether Joshua Smith or the woman
Elizabeth should go with them, but instead they
had been shown the house and then gone up to
it alone. Elizabeth was to come as the occasion
demanded. It was one of the Swiss chalet types
with a steeply sloping roof and drooping eaves; a
"pretty" house with an enormous beech tree just
behind it, one branch almost touching the roof.

Mary Lee-Wilberforce had opened the door
and said:

"Oh! I didn't expect strangers."

"Are you Mary Wilberforce?" Hardy had asked formally.

"Yes, I am. I—oh! Dr. Cellini, I didn't recognise you, the sun was in my eyes. Please come in." The room had a picture window from which could be seen the Patriarch's home.

"Mrs. Wilberforce—" Hardy had begun, and then wondered what was the matter with him. It was the steadfastness of the girl's expression of course; a kind of trusting. She had such a nice face, such soft-looking lips, such a creamy throat.

Throat.

"Mary," Cellini had said. "I have some distressing news for you."

"Distressing?" Her brow had furrowed.

"Yes, very."

"I don't understand you," she said, but it was not with perversity; it was simple fact.

"Lionel didn't come home last night," Cellini had said, quietly.

"I know." Perhaps a hint of laughter had shown in her eyes because both question and answer had been so obvious. "He does stay away, sometimes. He—"

"He—" began Cellini, then broke off. "Go on."

"I am afraid he is no longer very happy with me," she went on simply. "If he were, he wouldn't leave so often."

"Mary," Cellini had said, taking her hands,

'Wife' and Mother   137

finding it difficult to break the news to her.
What was it about this girl? What was it about
others here? A kind of naturalness, Hardy
thought, both then and afterwards. He was still
unable to put his finger on it. "The news is simply this: Lionel won't ever be back. He was—he
died last night."

She echoed, as if not understanding: "Died?"

"I'm afraid so, my dear." Cellini had never
looked more distressed.

"*Dead*," she repeated in a sighing voice.

"Yes, Mary. He—I hate to tell you this, but he
was murdered."

The tension was almost unbearable, because
she simply did not appear to be taking in what
Cellini said: it was as if she had not heard. Cellini
had tightened his hold perceptibly and gone on:

"Do you understand, Mary?"

"Understand?"

"Lionel was murdered last night. Murdered,
at Pucklebury Ring. Did you—did you know he
was going out of the Community last night?"

"No," she replied, and paused. Then: "No. He
did not tell me where he was going and I did not
ask him because I thought he would think me
possessive. I did not—I did not want to lose
him." She went off into a kind of reverie; dazed
and yet reflective. "You—you say he is dead?"

"Yes," Cellini had said. "He was—"

That was the moment when she had changed
her expression, drawn herself up, looked about

her desperately. Her eyes had the fire which had shown in Elizabeth's, not long ago, but there was an added quality: desperation. She had looked past Cellini towards the lawns and the trees, then said in a gasping voice:

"I must see my children."

She had moved past them and opened the door. Elizabeth, standing nearby, took a step towards her and then drew back. For Mary Wilberforce broke into a run. She ran very easily and quickly, towards a building Hardy had seen but not really noticed before. When she reached level ground she ran faster, and as the men had hurried outside to watch, they saw children playing: a dozen or more of them, with two women watching. Mary ran to one of the children, boy or girl they couldn't see, and bent down and picked the child up, then looking wildly about, ran again to a younger child, a toddler. She hoisted this one, effortlessly, and, carrying the pair, walked off.

Only a few hours later, when it was not much after six o'clock, this same Mary was supervising her own children and the children of the Community as they played.

"Mary," Cellini said, "we must ask you some questions."

"Of course," she said. "I am all right now."

"They may be painful, I'm afraid."

"It is all painful," she replied.

They were outside her chalet in the cool of the evening; it would soon be chilly. A few people were about in the distance and from somewhere the twanging notes of a guitar sounded, but nothing really obtruded on the quiet. It was, reflected Hardy, quite the strangest investigation he had conducted, anywhere.

"Mary," he said, "did your husband have any enemies?"

"I think he had many," she answered.

"Men? Were they men?"

"Yes," she answered simply. "The men whose wives he had used."

"So you knew about that."

"Am I blind?" she asked simply. "Yes, I knew from the beginning."

"Was he frightened of any one man in particular, do you know?"

"He said that all men here were cowards who would do nothing to protect their women."

"And he was afraid of none."

"No," she answered, obviously having no doubt at all. "He had no fear."

"Yet someone killed him."

"You told me that he had been killed. Elizabeth told me later that he was strangled," she said, and looked down at her hands.

She held them as Joshua Smith had held his: in front of her breasts and palms downwards on a slight slant. It was as if she wanted to place them round some object; a throat? The fingers

curled a little; they actually moved as if pulled by
some invisible strings. Then she lowered them
and said to Hardy:

"It was an evil thing to do."

"He had done what many believe to be evil,"
Cellini remarked softly.

"There is no evil worse than taking a human
life," she responded flatly.

"Do you know anyone who threatened him?"
Hardy asked.

"No."

"Or anyone who was ever violent towards
him?"

"No," she repeated.

"Did anyone hate him?"

"Someone must have but I do not know who."
She looked down at her hands again but this
time there was no tension in them; no nervous
strength.

"Did you ever see anyone follow him from
here at night?" asked Hardy.

"I know of no one," she answered. "I did not
spy on him. His life was his own."

"Did you resent being left alone?" Hardy
wanted to know.

She looked at the detective and there was a
pity in her voice as well as an expression which
seemed to say that she could not really understand such a remark. She glanced at Cellini as if
expecting him to comment, but he simply
watched her.

"I was never left alone," she answered.

"But he often left you," protested Hardy.

"That is not leaving me alone. There are always people here, that is one of the great benefits of Merryfield. One's friends, who are as close as one's family. Here, one is never lonely even if one is sometimes alone. I enjoy being by myself some of the time, as well as being with others, by myself or with Lionel." She was speaking as if her "husband" were alive, and the expression in her eyes was peaceful; did it reflect peace in her heart? "Sometimes I do not understand you people from outside," she went on with a touch of impatience, and her voice was much stronger, anger sparked in her eyes. "You make marriage a cage out there. Your conventions force two people to marry and then you lock them up together so that they can have no pleasure in the company of others. So, they come to hate each other. Oh, I know, I *know*. My own mother and father so hated each other that once he tried to kill her!"

She paused, as if the very thought had made her bitterly angry, taking away the peace which had been within her only a few moments ago.

"And when you have put them in this cage and they have children, what follows? The children make the prison worse. Parents cannot get away from children or the four walls which shut them in, and the children are prisoners, too. You kill their spirit, creating hatred and deceit and dishonesty and prostitution and sickness. It is horrible," she cried. "Horrible!"

The word fell away to silence, and she said nothing more. Hardy could not decide which of a dozen things he wanted to ask, and later he admitted ruefully, for a few moments he was tongue-tied. He glanced at Cellini and it was a relief when Cellini spoke.

"Mary," he said, "any place is a cage if you wish to get out but cannot."

"I know!" she cried. "That is why the Community is so free, that is why I am happy for Lionel to do anything that makes him happy."

"What he did made someone hate him enough to want him dead and to kill him," declared Cellini. "You did not keep him here and he took pain and distress to others." She did not answer but seemed struck dumb, wild-eyed but helpless. And she watched and listened, breathless, as he went on: "He went from the Community last night and he made love to Carol Smith, and afterwards—"

She sprang forward, not letting him finish. She clenched her fists and shook them, her whole body aquiver as Elizabeth's had been while Joshua Smith had held her, comfortingly, only a few hours ago. This girl was suddenly, awfully, transformed. Lips twisted, her whole face distorted, she shook her fists within a few inches of his face.

"Why don't you question *Carol*? She knows where he went. She knows who hates him. She is the creature of the devil who is destroying the Community, destroying Lionel, destroying us all!"

11

Viper in the Bosom?

FOR A MOMENT it looked as if Mary Wilberforce was so possessed by fury that she would strike Cellini; strike anyone who was near her. Hardy made an instinctive move forward to protect the older man, but Cellini did not move at all, simply stared into her blazing eyes. Her fists still shook and her body quivered but she did not strike. Her breathing was harsh and heavy, as if she was fighting for life. The colour had gone from her cheeks and her pallor was alarming.

Then, to Hardy's astonishment, Cellini said sharply: "That was a wicked thing to say."

"Wicked!" Mary gasped. "She's the spawn of the devil!"

"Stop talking like that! She is the Patriarch's daughter."

"She is the spawn of the devil! Her mother was a whore!"

The door behind her opened and Joshua Smith stepped into the room while behind him came Elizabeth, calm and unflurried. Mary heard the opening of the door and spun round, only to back a pace when she saw who it was. Alarm—or was it *fear?*—sent a spasm across her face.

"Mary," Smith said gently. "Both Dr. Cellini and you are wrong. You have said nothing wicked, nothing which the shock and anxiety don't explain." He gave Cellini a reproving look as he touched the girl's hand. "In fact you have behaved astonishingly well in view of all that has happened. But you are wrong about Carol. She is as good a person as you. When you are calmer, you will realise that." He raised a hand to Elizabeth who moved to Mary's other side. "Will you look after her, Elizabeth, and see that she rests?"

"Of course," Elizabeth said.

Hardy, so used to Cellini's devious ways, so used to his changes of expression and almost able to read his mind, knew exactly what he wanted now. And he, Hardy, wanted the same thing. As Elizabeth turned, the girl made to follow her, and Hardy said:

"Don't go yet, please."

"My dear Superintendent, the child is in a state of—"

"I need to talk to her, Mr. Smith. To find out exactly what she meant when she called your daughter a creature of the devil and accused her mother—"

"Mary is distraught!" Smith interrupted, and with an imperious wave of his hand and in the manner of one who was used to having his own way, he went on: "Take her to my house, Elizabeth. Superintendent, I must talk with you."

"Mr. Smith," Hardy said in a firm voice. "I have exerted myself to be helpful, largely because of my long knowledge of and respect for Dr. Cellini, rather than any particular concern for you and the Community. But I am a policeman, and as a policeman I need to question Mary Wilberforce."

"And later you may," Smith said. "Elizabeth—"

"Mr. Smith," Hardy said, "I can question her here and now, or I can take her to the police station and question her there. The choice is yours."

"To remove her would be unforgivable!"

"And without stretching the law too far I could take you to the station for questioning, also," Hardy said sharply.

"You—you would not *dare*!"

"Oh, wouldn't I?" Hardy rasped. "You have a

curiously exaggerated view of your authority.'
He turned to the window, and raised his right
hand. Immediately two police officers who had
ostensibly been studying some tracks in the
grass, came hurrying. As he turned back to the
room, Elizabeth gripped the girl's arm and
pulled her towards the open door. Hardy sprang
forward but Smith, with obvious deliberation
impeded him. Elizabeth was already out of the
room, Mary, dragged willy-nilly, was in the doorway. Cellini made a move towards her. Hardy attempted to sweep Smith aside, but found him as
resistant as a rock. Cellini stepped past them
both and then pushed past the girl.

They were in a smaller kitchen, with a wide
window over-looking a clearing and the back
and sides of other houses. The room was spick
and span, the table a huge slab of wood polished
like most of the wood in this place.

On it lay a hypodermic syringe, very like the
one which the nurse had used on Carol Smith.

Mary gasped: "No. No!"

Elizabeth actually made a movement towards
the syringe but she must have realised that it was
too late, so she did not touch it. Joshua Smith
was coming through the doorway now, angry-
faced, Hardy just behind him, the two detectives
only a few feet behind him in turn. Cellini thrust
out his hand and picked up the box, closing the
lid before Hardy had a chance to see what it was.
Then he stood aside, slipping the box into his

pocket. Smith and Elizabeth looked at him in astonishment and relief. Hardy strode in, flinging words over his shoulder:

"Wait there. Let no one pass."

"Sir," one of the policemen acknowledged.

"Now what the devil do you think you're playing at?" Hardy rasped. Cellini, knowing him so well, realised that his anger was actually ebbing but that he would not want to let the others see that. "The quicker all of you are at the station the better. This is a *police* enquiry, and I have a warrant to search these premises and grounds and the right to detain anyone who gives me sufficient cause." When no one spoke and even Smith seemed genuinely shocked, he went on harshly. "I ought to charge you with obstructing a police officer in the execution of his duty. A night in a cell and a hearing in the court tomorrow might cool you down."

"Oh, God!" breathed Elizabeth. "Oh, no!"

Smith was gaping at Hardy, and there was no doubt of his alarm, but he was breathing hard and in this crisis did not seem to be able to find words. Mary dropped on to a kitchen chair and buried her face in her hands, while Cellini stood by her, a hand at her shoulder.

"No, please no," Elizabeth begged.

"Give me one good reason why I shouldn't."

"It would—it would do such harm."

"To whom? *You?* This man you call the Patriarch? Or Mary—or who?"

"To the whole Community."

"*This* Community or the larger one outside?"

"Oh, please," Elizabeth pleaded. "Please don't let it happen. Joshua and I—" she broke off but soon repeated: "Joshua and I simply wanted to help Mary. She has had such a terrible time."

"You mean you wanted to prevent us from questioning her."

"Only—only until she had rested," Elizabeth said. "That was all. She has had such a terrible experience."

"At whose hands?" barked Hardy.

"At—at her husband's."

"You mean the man she was living with here and who was murdered in cold blood last night?"

"We regarded him as her husband."

"No one else would." Hardy spun round on Smith, who, deathly pale, was watching and listening, breathing through parted lips, while his forehead was beaded with sweat, which ran into his eyes making it seem as if they were swimming. "Now, sir! What is it you want to prevent Mary from saying? Why are you so anxious we should not question her? Come on: out with it! I *can* charge you with obstruction, you know."

"Joshua," Elizabeth said, imploringly. "Don't let them take you away."

Smith moistened his lips.

Cellini felt the girl relax a little, as if she needed physical support. He did not move or disturb her. He had seen Hardy at work often, and always with a mixture of admiration and surprise. For so much of the time he acted almost as a spectator, allowing himself—or so it seemed—to be pushed around. Then, at the moment it was least expected, he became an aggressive policeman adjusting himself to the circumstances, using exactly the right tactics for each particular occasion.

Now, he said: "I want an answer at once. If I don't get it I shall take all three of you to the police station and make a statement to the Press saying that I think you can help us with our enquiries. *What don't you want Mary to tell us?*"

That was the moment when Mary looked up.

She looked at Joshua Smith, not at Elizabeth who was so distraught. She said in a husky voice:

"He didn't want me to admit I left the Community last night."

"Mary," Elizabeth choked. "Mary!"

"He made me promise not to," Mary said in the same quavering voice. "He made me promise to lie to you."

Very much more gently, Hardy said: "So you did go out last night."

"Yes. Yes, I did."

"Following your husband?"

"Yes."

"To Pucklebury Ring?"

"Yes."

"Did you see whom he met?" Now Hardy's voice was touched with compassion while

Cellini's left hand rested on the girl's shoulder as she moved away from him for the first time, and said in a quiet voice:

"He saw Carol."

"Are you sure?"

"Yes. I actually saw them meet."

"Was anyone else there with them?"

"No."

"Can you be sure of that?"

"I can only be sure that I saw no one else as I followed them," Mary said, and Cellini pressed her shoulder again, reassuringly, congratulatingly.

"How long did you stay?"

Bitterly, Mary answered: "Long enough!"

"How long does that mean?" enquired Hardy.

Joshua Smith interpolated in a broken voice, a voice which told of hopelessness and acute distress, of a man whose will and whose strength had been sapped until there was very little left.

"Don't—please don't go on."

"Please do not interrupt," Hardy ordered.

"It is torture!"

"If you can't stand it, go outside. Mary—" Not once had Hardy looked away from the girl, and when he spoke to her his tone changed from harshness to mildness: "How long did you stay watching your husband with Carol?"

"I—I don't know," she said. "I don't know. I—" she raised a hand and placed it in Cellini's. "I—I felt as if I couldn't move. I couldn't believe it was happening. They—they met near the big oak tree, and—and they walked off hand-in-hand. They didn't kiss or hug each other, they just walked towards the Ring. And—and into a hollow. I was on the bank, looking down. I went down on my knees and I tried to pray but I couldn't. They—they lay down together. It was *awful*. I saw everything. I *saw* my husband—" She was gripping Cellini's hand very tightly now as the words came slowly and wonderingly, as if she was telling not what she *had* seen but what she was seeing at this moment: and she made the scene so vivid that no one could fail to see and to understand.

"Did you see anyone nearby?" Hardy asked again.

"I was obsessed by them, I know of nothing else," Mary replied. "Usually when I walk out by night I see and hear the little animals, I hear many sounds, but last night there was nothing but them. At first they just walked hand-in-hand. I wasn't near anough to hear what they said. Their heads were close together. Sometimes, Lionel—Lionel laughed. I knew he was happy. That was the most awful thing, he was *happy*. He wasn't pretending. He—he always told me that he went with other women because he had such a strong sexual urge. He said it was purely—purely physical. He would laugh and call it *lust*! He said that when it was over he lost all interest, and the woman didn't matter any more.

"But he was happy last night.

"I knew she had made him love her.

"I knew—I knew that I had lost him.

"When they lay down together I wanted to go away but—but I couldn't. My body wouldn't move, it was as if I was paralysed. I saw—everything. There was—there was enough starlight to show me. It fell upon them. It made them like creatures from another world. It played on their legs, it—"

"For God's sake stop!" cried Joshua Smith, and now he moved towards the child, hands outstretched towards her. As he drew close he crouched as if he would go down on his knees. The sweat was flowing down his cheeks and into his beard, his eyes were swimming in sweat: or were they tears? He did not touch her as he pleaded: "Mary! You musn't think about it, it was all a nightmare, a terrible dream. You mustn't think about it."

Cellini felt the small hand tighten even more in his. He felt her body tighten as if she were keying herself up to speak. Except for Smith's laboured breathing and her breathing, too, there seemed no sound.

"It wasn't a nightmare. It was real."

"Mary, I beg you—"

"It was real," repeated Mary in a quiet voice, "and you want me to pretend it was a nightmare."

"It will fade, Mary, it will fade like nightmares do," he promised as if swearing an oath.

"Perhaps it will," she conceded. She seemed withdrawn, and spoke without emotion but with a sense which might be wonder and might be a kind of distaste. "But it was real and you don't want to admit it. You *never* want to admit anything that is bad and evil, do you?"

"Mary!" he choked.

"You are always talking to us about truth and beauty, but when it comes to ugly things you just want to close your eyes to them," she said. "And you want to close our eyes to this, also. Well, my eyes are open, *wide* open. Your way doesn't work. It's an awful failure. You've made a kind of make-believe world and it looks good to you because you simply won't believe in the bad. You've told *me* that true love can withstand everything, that after a while the way Lionel behaved would stop hurting, but it never stopped. It always hurt. And I think you know it did," she went on, speaking very softly. "I think you yourself are so sensitive to pain that you just have to put on a kind of armour and pretend that it doesn't exist. You live a lie, don't you? There is a viper in your bosom. You talk and act as if you are a fighter, you made so many of us believe in a good life, a perfect life here, but it's all a lie. Like telling me last night was a nightmare, and trying to make me lie about it. When you came here early this afternoon and told me the police were here and that I was not to tell them I had been out last night, you tried to persuade me that was a good lie. But it wasn't. It was the worse because you have always taught us to worship the truth."

She finished with the word 'truth' uttered in a tone of infinite sadness as she looked into Joshua Smith's tormented face; at a torment there for all to see.

12

Torment

ELIZABETH, WHOSE OTHER namé they did not know, was the first to move. She straightened up and crossed slowly to Joshua Smith, who was staring in that tormented way at the girl, little more than a child, who had uttered such a damning indictment. She touched Smith's hand, but he did not appear to notice. The movement broke the tension, and Cellini squeezed Mary's hand for a moment, then released her. She looked away from Smith to Cellini.

"I'm sorry," she said.

"You have nothing to be sorry about," he assured her.

She looked at Hardy, and repeated: "I am sorry I lied to you."

"What matters now is that you have told us the truth," Hardy assured her. He sent a side-long glance at Joshua Smith as he went on: "I shall need to talk to you again. Would you rather stay here, or—"

"No!" she exclaimed. "I would like to leave."

"But Mary," Elizabeth protested, "where can you go?"

"I know of someone with whom she can stay and be at peace," Cellini put in quickly. "Don't worry about her safety." He looked at Hardy and went on: "I would like to take her myself, John—or perhaps send Scobie with her."

"Scobie," Hardy said, without adding the obvious, that he would like Cellini to remain here. He moved towards the main room, saying to Smith as he passed: "I'd like a little more time with you, sir, but I will try not to keep you long." He went into the bigger room, where Scobie stood up from the flat wooden arm of a chair. He had a notebook in one hand, a ball-point pen in the other. "Did you get Mary Wilberforce's statement?" asked Hardy.

"Practically verbatim, sir—in fact I think I have all the conversation."

"And I've a memory like a tape-recorder," volunteered the other man, whom Hardy hadn't met. "I can help prepare a typewritten version, sir, if I see a transcription within twenty-four hours."

"Good," Hardy said. "Who are you?"

"Sergeant Bowles, sir, Halling Division."

"I'd like Mr. Scobie to make the report your next job," Hardy said, "immediately after you've taken Mrs. Wilberforce to the station."

"Sir," said Scobie, obviously wanting to comment.

"Yes."

"If Dr. Cellini's suggestion is to take Mrs. Wilberforce out of the district, then—"

"I'm sure it won't be," Hardy interrupted. "But what would you suggest?"

"Woman Police Constable Bessington," answered Scobie, eagerly. "She has a small flat where there's plenty of room for a day or two, and it's possible that—" Scobie broke off in some confusion, and added awkwardly. "Sorry, sir,"

"What were you going to say?" asked Hardy.

"Well, sir, Bess is quite a remarkable person in many ways, especially at winning confidences," Scobie answered. "I just thought—" He broke off again.

"Well, don't keep it to yourself," Hardy urged.

"If I were in charge, sir, which I know I'm not and I hope I'm not presuming, I would assign W.P.C. Bessington to the task of encouraging both Mrs. Wilberforce and Carol Smith to talk," Scobie blurted out. "And that would be a pretty full-time job."

"It sounds like it," Hardy conceded.

"But—" began Scobie, only to break off again.

Hardy had never met the detective inspector

before, but what he had seen of him today he
had liked. This was the first time Scobie had
shown any sign of dithering, and clearly he was
troubled and did not quite know what to say.
Possibly it was because the man Bowles was present. Certainly Bowles was standing there in an
almost predatory fashion as if waiting to interrupt; and clearly the sergeant had a good conceit
of himself and his memory. He was a big, heavy
man.

"Sergeant," Hardy said, "go and ask Dr.
Cellini if he can spare me a moment, and then
stay with Mr. Smith and the woman, Elizabeth,
until I come back."

Bowles was eager: "Right, sir!"

"And make a mental note of anything they
say," added Hardy.

"I'll do that, sir, never fear!"

Scobie, despite his dithering and his problem,
could not conceal a smile as Bowles went off eagerly. No one in the kitchen appeared to be talking; and no one appeared to have moved. Hardy
moved towards the front door and opened it,
and suddenly his thoughts were distracted from
what had happened and from what he had
wanted to say to Scobie.

For the scene outside was so unexpécted.

Instead of the police moving about and a few
of the members of the Community also,
including two groups of children in their play-
grounds, at least a hundred people had gath-

ered, men and women who looked young or middle-aged. Most of these were in pairs. All of them had gathered near the clearing between the big buildings and the individual houses. Some were sitting on the grass. There was nothing aggressive in their manner but they made a half-circle through which it would be difficult to pass unless several of them moved aside. Two knots of policemen were at either side, as if assessing the situation and not knowing what to make of it. On one side, as if making it clear that he was neither of the police nor of the Community there was a youngish man with very red hair; Hardy recognised him as a reporter from one of the more popular Fleet Street newspapers with a circulation of several millions.

"What's going on?" asked Hardy.

"I don't know, sir," Scobie answered. "I was so intent on what was being said in the kitchen that I didn't even glance out of the window. I should say—" he broke off.

"Don't dither so much," Hardy said, sharply.

"No, sir," Scobie said, almost humbly. He scanned the crescent of people as he went on: "I recognize several of the members of the Community, and it's after six o'clock. It looks as if the men who work outside during the day have come home and brought their families out to see what's going on."

"Yes," Hardy said, heavily. "I've never met anything quite like this before, either. Well, leave that for a moment. What's on your mind, Inspector? You seem to have a lot, and also seem reluctant to say it."

"I'm sorry, sir."

"What were you trying to say inside there?"

Scobie turned away from the crowd of members obviously to concentrate on the senior detective from New Scotland Yard. Hardy studied the well-marked features, the narrow, curiously spade-like jaw, the small mouth. There was a similarity between him and the policewoman Bessington, although she was much more striking. Scobie's most impressive feature was his eyes, a clear brown, darker than hazel, lighter than chestnut. They were not only intent but, Hardy thought, pleading.

"May I speak freely, sir?"

"Of course."

"I *am* inclined to take initiative in some ways."

"You wouldn't be an inspector if you weren't."

"Thank you, sir. But it isn't always easy here at Halling, and I don't want to blot my copybook with a senior officer such as yourself."

"You'll fill it with blots if you don't tell me what's on your mind," Hardy growled.

He thought afterwards that he should not have needed telling; or at least, he should have had some idea of what was worrying Scobie. But he hadn't. It may have been because of the high drama of the past half-hour; of the swift turn of events; of his awareness of the tensions and emotions, the hurts and the hatreds which hovered over this place; as well as the danger which might well exist to others and the fact that a murderer had to be caught. Whatever the reasons, Scobie's next words took him completely by surprise.

"This isn't the best division for initiative," Scobie stated.

"One can take the initiative one moment and be praised, take it the next and be bawled out. I hope this doesn't sound disloyal, sir."

Hardy, shaken, looked at him very steadily, and at last realised that he should have known what was troubling the man. He already knew of Atkinson's irascibility, and that the Halling Superintendent had moods of great strength as well as prejudices which made him unyielding at times. But he, Hardy, had felt that this was probably due to the fact that a Yard man had come down and virtually usurped his job where the Community was concerned. In fact, Hardy had felt almost guilty about it. He had no sense of guilt, now, but of wariness. He must be careful what he said; must neither over-encourage Scobie nor dampen him too much.

"What in particular has made you raise this now?" he enquired. He glanced at the crowd and saw that a few more couples, some with children, were moving towards the big party, but there were no more policemen and no more reporters as far as he could tell. He noticed this, and also

saw Cellini appear, the girl by his side, and stand
and watch the silent people.

He sensed for the first time a kind of uncertainty. Of tension. It would be too much to call it
menace, but certainly it was strange. But his
main concern was with Scobie, who had gone
very red.

"I think it's very urgent, sir, or I wouldn't have
raised it. I know Mr. Atkinson is going to retire
in a few months' time but—" he drew himself up
virtually to attention and went on in a brisker
voice: "I have reason to believe the Superintendent disapproves of Woman Police Constable
Bessington's report on Carol Smith and intends
to reject her request for a transfer to the C.I.D. I
think that could be a grave mistake, sir. I think
Bess can help us very materially to find out
what's happening here. That's all, sir. No insub-
ordination is intended, I assure you."

"I am quite sure there isn't," Hardy replied reassuringly. "Leave the matter to me, Inspector."

"Yes, sir. Thank you, sir."

Hardy half-turned.

Cellini, standing within earshot had Hardy
spoken loudly, moved towards him, with Mary
close by his side. She had changed from the
short toga-like dress into a green sheath with
half-length sleeves and a hem-line well above the
knee. She carried a green leather handbag and
wore shoes, not sandals, to match. Now, she

stared as if anxiously at the half-circle of members.

"John," Cellini said, "how long have they been there?"

"Probably for half an hour," Hardy answered. He felt curiously at a loss, as he studied the silent multitude. "Multitude" was too strong a word but there were certainly over two hundred now. "I wonder if they've a spokesman," he mused aloud.

"Or what they want," said Cellini.

It was obvious from the way he spoke that he did not like this situation at all, and his reaction affected Hardy, who for the first time felt a sense of silent menace. He tried to tell himself that he was being absurd: these were not violent people, they would offer no danger. In any case what kind of danger did he expect? No one would attack the police.

His heart began to beat faster at the realisation that the words had formed in his mind; and they could only have been born out of fear. Good God! There were twenty or more policemen on the grounds, it was utterly ridiculous to think of an attack.

But he *had* thought of one.

"Mary," Cellini said, "do you know what they want?"

"I know what they *might* want," she answered, and stopped.

"What?" asked Hardy, too sharply.

"They might want you to leave Merryfield," she said. "They hate any kind of intrusion. We are such a self-contained community. I've known—" She hesitated, but went on without prompting: "I've known something like this before."

"When?" asked Hardy, more quietly. "And why?"

"It was a year ago," she answered in a low-pitched voice. "Perhaps—perhaps two. Joshua wanted a man to be banished from the Community and they did not want him to go."

"*Did* he go?"

"Yes," Mary said.

"What happened?" Hardy demanded.

"They told Joshua that if he insisted on banishment they would leave the Community," she answered. "But he sent the man away and told them they must do what their consciences told them. If they thought him wrong, then he himself would go and they must appoint another Patriarch." She watched the ranks of the members closely and her voice sharpened: "They sent a spokesman to ask him to stay, and—there is the spokesman, now. The same man, coming toward us."

The man who came towards the house was a red-haired newspaperman who had been outside the police station when Cellini had left.

He walked with long, deliberate steps and

looked not unlike a monk or friar. He brought with him a strange but unmistakable aura of menace, even of evil. His hair and milk-pale face made him stand out against the others. He made no sound, and except for the noises of the nearby countryside and far-off lowing of cattle, there was no sound. The two knots of policemen did not move; they were standing between the main body of the crowd and Hardy, Cellini, Mary and Scobie.

He drew within twenty yards before he spoke.

"Chief Superintendent Hardy, my name is Samuel Ryall. I would like to talk to you."

Hardy had to make an effort to say: "What about, please?"

"Obviously, about the situation here," replied the man with red hair. "I am speaking for the Community as the Patriarch is not at this moment able to speak for us." When Hardy made no comment, he went on: "No murder was committed in these grounds last night. No one here has committed a crime, as far as we know or have been told. We do not want you here any longer. If you wish for information we will come to give it to you at police headquarters, but we will not permit this intrusion on our privacy. Nor," he went on in a carrying voice, "will we permit you to take any of our members, whether it be the Patriarch or Elizabeth, Mary or any other man or woman in this sanctuary. If they are to be punished we shall punish them."

He paused for a long time, looking more intently at Hardy now than at Mary, and when he went on it was in an incisive voice.

"You may go in peace. Leave us to ours. But you may not take Mary nor any other member."

Ryall moved farther back towards the crowd but faced the smaller group of visitors all the time, obviously waiting for a reply, as obviously expecting it to be hostile. The men and women behind him did not move and did not make a sound. Hardy saw now that all the children had gone, only adults were here. There could be little doubt that they agreed with what the red-haired man said; that he spoke for them all.

"Go in peace," had sounded like a blessing.

"If they are to be punished we shall punish them," meant exactly what it said. These people were asserting their right to judge their members and to punish them, irrespective of the law of the land. The incredible thing was that they so obviously meant this utter defiance: meant to provoke a conflict with the law.

13

Evasion

DR. CELLINI HAD the strongest feeling that the situation had reached flash-point. He had not for one moment anticipated that it would come so soon; he had feared it might come eventually and saw exactly why. In one way it was unavoidable; no one in the Community, not even Joshua Smith, had absolute authority; it was vested in the members. Over the years, Merryfield had established its own customs, traditions, even its own laws. Ryall used the perfect word: it had become a sanctuary for those who wanted, so far as it was practicable, to withdraw from the society which surrounded them.

Indeed, the Merryfield Community, like so many others, had been founded for just that

purpose: to be a sanctuary for those who re-
belled against society. One could think, as many
did, that for many it was a withdrawal from responsibility to the world; one could call it cow-
ardly; one could say that Community members
who never left Merryfield were burying their
heads in the sand of their own oblivion. Whatever was said, for or against, it could not be
denied that it was an experiment in living and
that many, like Joshua Smith, were trying desperately hard to create a free society.

Many societies had been tried and had failed.

From the great experiment of Robert Owen,
some two hundred years ago, to the latest community such as this, countless attempts had
failed. But in his extensive knowledge of them,
culled out of general reading and concentrated
study since Smith had come to him, Cellini had
not heard of one which had come so near crisis:
so near flash-point.

For what could Hardy do?

He could not, as a policeman, allow this man
or these people to tell him how he could act. This
was England, and the law was the law and the
upholders of it must show no weakness. Had this
man come to him and explained, and asked for
understanding, then Hardy would have done
everything he could to help: no man at Scotland
Yard applied human values to the heartless routine of crime investigation more than John
Hardy.

But what could he do now? Cellini asked himself again, and he was as near frightened and indeed as near hopeless as he had ever been. He
watched Hardy closely and saw no sign of anger
or impatience; under pressure he was always at
his best. There was tension of a kind among the
other policemen, though, and Cellini saw what
he hadn't noticed before; another group was
gathered in the place where the cars were
parked. They could call for help, of course, but
once they did this, the open conflict which he,
Cellini, wanted at all costs to avoid, would be inescapable. What a heyday the newspapers would
have!

Hardy was a long time responding; it was almost as if he were nonplussed. And the tension
grew, heightened by the stillness. No one moved,
not even the policemen. Some distance off, from
out of sight, a child began to laugh and the
sound was startlingly loud.

It was Hardy's signal to speak; and his first
question was completely unexpected.

"As you speak for everyone, sir, may I know
your name? I didn't catch it."

Immediately, the red-haired man answered:
"Ryall. Samuel Ryall."

"Thank you, Mr. Ryall. And—forgive me—
but to convince myself that you *do* speak for all
the members present, may we have a show of
hands? If there are any dissenters, this is surely
the time to find out." Hardy's smile came

quickly, freely; he was rather like a small boy suddenly and unexpectedly enjoying himself. Cellini's anxiety began to ease but his curiosity expanded enormously. "Will you all put up—" he raised his own right hand.

Immediately a forest of hands went up, and with the movement there was a break in the tension. Two or three of the members smiled. Hardy made a little play of moving his head right and left as if to see everybody, then raised both hands in a gesture of acceptance.

"Thank you. Mr. Ryall, until a short while ago I thought that Joshua Smith spoke for you all. Isn't he your spokesman any longer?"

"When he is free to, he may be," Ryall answered.

"Why isn't he free?"

"His daughter had been partly the cause of what has happened, answered Ryall, "and it is not right that a man under such emotional pressure should have to shoulder such responsibility."

"Is he aware of this?" asked Hardy.

"It is accepted," Ryall replied. "No one questions it, least of all the Patriarch."

"I see," Hardy said, but now he frowned and hesitated for a few moments, glancing at Cellini as if puzzled, appeared to be running the risk of allowing the mood of the members to harden again, but then went on in what might have been an aside but in a carrying voice: "So at a time of

crisis the members themselves take control. Yes."
He raised his voice, and his tone and his manner
changed but there was no aggressiveness in his
manner although there was authority. "I think
you should all know this. Nothing we have yet
found here could justify us in making an arrest
or even taking any members to the police station
for questioning. If such a situation existed, of
course, I would have no choice but to take them.
I repeat: it doesn't." He must have been aware of
the way many of the members relaxed, an easing
of the tension in a way that hadn't seemed possible a few minutes before, but he did not pause,
simply went on in that manner of brisk authority. "However, we have indisputable evidence of
one unpalatable fact. One of your number has
been murdered. It's conceivable that others are
in danger. If you doubt it, hear this. Carol Smith
was near the scene of the crime; I needn't go into
reasons at this stage. So was Mary Wilberforce.
Each could have seen the murderer, and so be
able to identify him. By some sign or sound he
may have betrayed himself in a way which one or
both of the young women may remember. So, he
may try to kill them. I do not think either of
these young women is safe here in Merryfield. I
cannot leave sufficient officers here night and
day to make sure they are safe, and I cannot allow the Community to accept the responsibility
of keeping them safe. So, I have no choice. For
their own safety I must ask Mary Wilberforce to

come into Halling with me, and I must keep
Carol Smith there. It is a good thing there are
two of them; one member on her own would feel
very isolated. The moment we have results, the
moment we feel it safe for them to return here
be sure we will bring them back. Meanwhile, the
police officers who have to stay here will cause as
little nuisance as they can."

It was strange to see the effect of his words;
the way the men and women moved about in re-
laxation; how several turned to each other and
smiled or spoke. Cellini was silently applauding
but at the same time watching the man Ryall very
closely. Hardy appeared not to look at Ryall or
anyone else except Mary. He gripped her hand
for a moment and then started off at a good pace
towards a gap which was now appearing in the
closed ranks. Some of the policemen moved into
the gap as if to make sure it was kept open, but
they need not have worried. Mary, scared,
looked about the crowd. Hardy simply raised his
right hand in a salute and called:

"I'll see you again, Mr. Ryall . . . Goodbye, all."
He did not appear to hustle Mary down to the
waiting cars but he certainly lost no time and
Cellini had some difficulty in keeping pace with
him. Soon they were getting into Scobie's car;
and Scobie was already by the open door.

"You stay and look after things here," Hardy
told him. "Don't change anything, just keep on
with questions, especially whether anyone was

seen coming back from the Common or leaving the Community after ten o'clock last night."

"There's a little thing you should know, sir. Ryall's always been a bit of a trouble-maker and he was once sent to prison for three months for being drunk and disorderly."

"He looks a tough customer," Hardy said. "Avoid conflict with him if you can. And if you get any impression that some of the members are lying or being evasive, let me or Mr. Atkinson know," Hardy went on. Then, getting into the car, he looked straight into Scobie's eyes and said: "I shall consider the other matter carefully."

"Thank you very much, sir."

"And be careful what you say in any of the houses or any of the meeting places, picnic spots and the amphitheatre," Hardy went on. "I don't yet know whether the place is wired so that a broadcast system can operate and reach every part of the village or whether any broadcast can only be picked up in one or two centres." He glanced over his shoulder into the car, and asked casually: "Do you know, Mary?"

She answered: "It depends which channel is used."

"You mean the Community *is* wired!" exclaimed Cellini. "Good gracious! It hadn't occurred to me!" He was utterly flabbergasted, and showed it.

Scobie, too, was clearly taken aback, although

he made no comment, simply waited for Hardy
to go on. Several other detectives, within earshot, stopped to look and listen. None of the
members had followed but were standing about
in small groups, or walking away in twos and
threes. Children began to appear from the chalets, too, and also stayed in groups.

"What channels are there?" Hardy asked
Mary.

"Two," she answered. "One is connected with
every chalet and every meeting place, so that
whatever is said in one place can be heard in all
the others. The second channel is simply used by
the Patriarch and from certain meeting places,
so that a general broadcast to people outside can
be made."

"I see," Hardy said. "Did you get that, Scobie?"

"Yes, sir."

"So be very careful nothing confidential is said
in a place where the words might be picked up
and relayed anywhere," Hardy emphasized. He
got into the car at last, sitting next to a youthful-
looking driver with a long, red neck, who started
the engine at once. They moved slowly down the
winding road, meeting no one on the way. But at
the entrance there was a crowd of at least a hundred people, only some of them reporters. A
dozen cars were drawn up on the grass verges of
the road and a policeman was guiding traffic
while two others were moving among the crowd,
obviously trying to persuade the people to move

on. They were not having much luck. Hardy made no comment as the policeman on traffic duty cleared a way for them; no comment until they were on the road which led across the Common. Then he turned and looked at the girl.

"How are you, Mary?" he asked.

"I feel shaky," she replied huskily.

"I can well understand it. After what you said about Carol Smith, do you want to be with her?"

After a long pause, Mary said in a low-pitched voice? "I don't know."

"What do you really think about her?"

"I—I don't know that, either."

"Did you mean what you said about her?"

"When I said it, yes, I did."

"But are you having second thoughts?"

"Yes. I—I lost my temper."

"And small wonder!" Hardy exclaimed. "I want you to understand that you don't have to be in the same place as Carol."

"I think—I think I would rather be on my own for tonight," Mary said. Her pale grey eyes, so wide-set, misted as with tears, and she leaned back in her corner.

Cellini was thinking, obviously she couldn't stay by herself tonight, but as obviously it *would* be a great risk to have her stay in the same room as Carol. The deep-rooted resentment, the jealously which this girl felt might well over-flow again with even greater force. He did not think this was the time to make any suggestion to

Hardy, who appeared to be thinking deeply and who had the situation well under control. In any case it would be difficult to discuss what to do while the girl was still with them.

The car drew up outside the police station and a man on duty came forward and opened the door. Both Cellini and Hardy moved to help Mary out but she needed no help. She stood, solitary, lonely, forlorn and so young, looking not at them but up at the open door of the police station.

Then, quite suddenly, she turned and ran.

Mary ran with deer-like swiftness, making hardly a sound, not looking behind her, long and sturdy legs moving so easily. She left all three men at a standing start and was yards away even before any of them moved. But the driver was still at the wheel, and hadn't yet switched off his engine. He leaned over and pulled one door, the policeman on duty slammed the other, the engine roared.

Hardy bellowed: "Don't hurt her!" and began to run after the girl.

The man on duty was only a step behind.

Cellini took two or three quick strides, and then came to a standstill. His heart was hammering, he was so afraid. He could catch only glimpses of the girl's legs. The police car had drawn level with her, and seemed to be going at terrifying speed. It turned towards the pave-

ment, obviously to cut her off, and the girl
seemed to put on an added spurt, as if to squeeze
between the front of the car and the wall of a
house alongside which she was running.

"Oh, dear God, dear God!" prayed Cellini.

*The girl, one moment going at full pelt, suddenly
stopped.*

She did not have to. There was room for her
to get by, had she kept going she would have
passed the car, but she stopped on that awful instant. The driver had misjudged by a yard or
more, and should have gone farther along, but
the front wheels of the car were mounting the
curb now, and the car was heading straight at the
girl.

She did not move.

She stood, her body pressed against the red-
brick wall, with the front of the car only a few
feet away from her. To Cellini, and to Hardy
and the duty policeman, both much closer, she
did not seem terrified. She made no attempt to
move but she could still fling herself to safety.
Her eyes were calm. Her lips were parted, and
moving as if in a prayer or incantation.

Cellini felt as if his heart would burst.

Hardy and the other man pulled up, only feet
from the car; if they had gone any farther they
must have crashed into it. The man in front of
Hardy actually flung out his arms as if to take
some of the inevitable impact on them. And
what happened seemed a miracle. As he thrust

his arms out the front of the car slewed round, as
if he had pushed it with a giant's strength. One
wheel, over the curb at that moment, clumped
off it as the driver turned his wheel desperately
The car, one wheel on and one wheel off the
pavement, stalled and stopped. There was a
wailing and screeching of brakes and a squealing
of rubber against the curb, but that was all.

The girl seemed to crumple up.

One moment she was spreadeagled against the
wall in the shape strangely like a person
crucified. The next all the strength seemed to
ooze from her body and she began to collapse.
Now it was Hardy who moved first, stopped her
held her against him for a moment as if in em-
brace, and then began to hoist her to his shoulders. The duty man said:

"Let me take her, sir." He took Mary and
placed her unceremoniously over his shoulder
and started back for the main entrance to the police station, where other officers had gathered
and some passers-by stood about. With Cellini in
front of him and Hardy a few yards behind he
said: "This way, sir," and turned as if on a reflex
action towards a small door which Cellini hadn't
noticed before. He pushed this open with one
hand and strode through, the girl still over his
shoulder, legs dangling, head dangling, too. On
the wall just inside a narrow passage was a sign
reading First Aid Room, and with another reflex

action the policeman pushed this door open and carried the girl inside.

A nurse, with a red cross on her starched white apron, stood up from a chair against the wall, and watched open-mouthed as the duty man placed the girl on a narrow bed.

Hardy saw all this; knew exactly what had to be done: leave the girl to the nurse for the time being, warn the nurse she might try to run away or injure herself, have another policewoman here on duty, have both door and window watched. But before he could speak, while he stood breathing hard and the man who had carried the girl stood taking in deep breaths, while Cellini watched, welcoming his role as spectator, foot-steps sounded along the passage, and Superintendent Atkinson appeared.

He looked at Cellini as if he were beneath contempt.

He stroke into the small first aid room, blocking the doorway.

He stood staring down at the girl on the narrow bed, her bright green dress vivid against the white of the sheets and pillow and bedspread. His lips worked. He gave the impression of being in the grip of ungovernable rage, that changed swiftly to signs of impending collapse.

The nurse cried: "Hold him!"

She spun round to a locker and pulled out a box with a hypodermic syringe, held it against the light to check that it was already primed, then gripped Atkinson's left wrist. The policeman and Hardy held the fat man, not against any struggles, just against his dead weight as he began to fall. She dabbed cotton wool into a tiny dish of pink liquid and rubbed the front of the forearm. Then with the speed and precision of long practice she drove the needle in. She withdrew it and dabbed at the puncture as a tiny globule of blood welled up, then pushed her chair into position and, with the men, helped the big, fat man into a sitting position.

His eyes were closed. He breathed stertorously. He overlapped the chair with each buttock. His hands flopped to his sides, almost touching the floor. His colour was purplish. When the nurse seemed sure he was comfortable as could be, she turned away and looked down at the girl on the narrow bed, who was staring fixedly at the ceiling.

"What—what's the matter with her?" she demanded.

"She is in a state of shock," Cellini stated in his quiet voice which sounded clearly above the heavy breathing of the others. "Nurse, how long has Mr. Atkinson been in this condition? Obviously he is in an acute state of diabetic collapse. How long have you been treating him in this way?"

14

Shock and Coma

Now it was Hardy's turn to be badly shaken by what he heard. Diabetes, of course; and Atkinson had almost gone into a coma! It explained a great deal: his bad temper, his unreasonableness, his changing moods, his prejudices. Any man who lived close to such an acute stage of diabetes lived in danger and existed on his nerves. And—my God, no wonder he was diabetic, with all that fat! He had little doubt that Cellini had realised what was the matter as soon as he had seen the man's behaviour, in much the same way as he—Hardy—had known that the Patriarch's house had been wired for a loudspeaker system when Smith had stared so fixedly at the wall above their heads.

Now, he was aware of a feeling of great relief.

Atkinson would have to go off duty for days if not weeks and Scobie and Robson would share the command. None of the problems of precedence and seniority would now be raised: he could use his own judgment without fear of giving offence. The feeling of relief soon faded in anxiety for Mary, who lay on her back with that fixed stare: trancelike. The nurse was feeling her pulse and Cellini was looking down at her intently. He was obviously tired and his shoulders sagged; he needed a long rest, or at least respite from tension. Yet the intentness in his expression was as great as ever; he seemed to be studying the girl's face but there was no way at all of guessing what was going on in his mind.

The nurse let the girl's arm go, and turned to Cellini.

"For about two years," she answered, belatedly.

"As seriously as this?"

"Yes, sir, quite as seriously."

"But surely—" began Cellini, and then broke off. "I am sorry, Nurse, this is an official matter and I am not here in an official capacity. What would you normally do now?"

"Send him home, sir."

"Send?" asked Hardy.

"Yes, sir," the nurse answered. She had sharp features, and a disagreeable expression, but her voice was pleasing enough. "Mr. Atkinson has me send for a special taxi, the one he uses himself since he stopped driving. It is large enough for him to get in and sit in comfortably, and the driver knows what to do. May I call for him now, sir?"

Hardy, looking at the fat man spread over the chair, said:

"Yes."

The nurse immediately dialled a number, and when she was answered, said: "Ask George to come to the police station as soon as he can, will you?" and rang off.

"So that's how you do it," remarked Hardy heavily. "He would be taken out by the side door, presumably."

"Yes, sir."

"And would any official report be made?"

"Only that Mr. Atkinson was indisposed, sir."

"How often has this kind of crisis occurred?" Hardy wanted to know.

"Not often, sir, Mr. Atkinson is usually most careful with his insulin and what he eats and drinks. But once every month or so he sort of bursts out, sir—he can't exert the self-discipline any longer. He *loves* his food and wine." Now the nurse's voice was positively gentle, and as obviously she was filled with concern. "And sometimes, when he gets worked up and excited or angry he will forget his injection and collapse, sir."

"Who else knows about this?" demanded Hardy.

The nurse hesitated, and then said uneasily: "I don't know."

"I see," Hardy said again. "I see." He saw the appeal in the nurse's eyes and studied her lined face closely. She was over made-up, and except for her eyes, not at all attractive. Yet she had one quality which would appeal particularly to most men: loyalty. She would not give any of the Uniform or C.I.D. staff away although some if not all must have known about this. There were a dozen questions he wanted to ask but wasn't at all sure he should ask her; what mattered was that she should be allowed to do her job as well as she could. But there was one thing he needed to know and which only the nurse could tell him.

He turned to the duty officer, and said: "I'll see you again in a few minutes, Constable. And—Good Lord! I'd forgotten that driver. Go and check, will you, see whether he was hurt and what damage there was to the car. I'll want to see him, too."

"Very good, sir." The man hurried out, big, clumsy-looking, untroubled. The nurse watched as if she were losing a friend and there was a scared expression in her eyes when she turned back to Hardy.

"We ought to do something with this young woman, sir."

"Very soon," Hardy interrupted. "Nurse, did Mr. Atkinson confide in you?"

"In what way, sir?" She looked even more apprehensive.

"Did he talk about personal things, particularly his likes and dislikes?" Hardy demanded, and then he added in a quiet, reassuring, even fatherly manner. "I shall keep anything you say in complete confidence, Nurse. You need not be afraid of Mr. Atkinson finding out or of anything being used to make things difficult for you." He gave her time to absorb this, and then went on: "Has he talked to you about retirement, for instance?"

Manny Cellini moved from the bed and sat on an upright chair near the door. He applauded, silently, but warmly. It was a long time since he had been as close as this to Hardy when he was working, and in many ways his friend had improved enormously. In a few minutes he would have this nurse talking, and what she said might be surprising, might even have a significant bearing on the Merryfield case. While he was thinking this he heard a car draw up outside, and saw the nurse look out of the window with its white net curtain.

"It's George," she said with relief.

In a moment "George" the taxi driver who

"knew what he had to do" came in with the big, cumbersome-looking policeman. Between them they hoisted Atkinson from the chair, and half-carried, half-dragged him out of the room. Very soon the car door slammed and the taxi moved off. The big man did not return immediately, and Cellini watched warily, wondering if the interruption had come at a bad time, and would discourage the nurse from talking.

"*Has* he talked to you about retirement?" Hardy asked, again; and he sounded as if there had been no interruption.

"Yes, often," she answered quietly. "He dreads the thought of it."

"Why?"

"He'll be so much on his own."

"Isn't he married?"

"He was, sir, but was divorced oh—fifteen or twenty years ago."

"Would he talk to you about any special anxieties?" enquired Hardy.

"He always keeps himself pretty well to himself, sir," the nurse answered. "He had a terrible blow when his marriage broke up, and he—well, he's never forgiven the man who took her away, or his wife either. I hope I'm not speaking out of turn, sir, but it made him very bitter, especially about certain things. I do know, sir; I probably know him better than anyone else."

When she said that there was a kind of defiance in her manner: as if she doubted whether they would believe her, yet nevertheless what she said was true.

"How well *do* you know him?" Hardy asked, gently.

The nurse said: "I *do* know him well." She paused. "You did mean it when you said this was absolutely in confidence, didn't you?"

"Of course," answered Hardy.

"Well, sir, we—Mr. Atkinson and I—have known each other for ten years or more now. We've never set up house together. I live in a house with my sister and her family and he has his apartment, he just can't bring himself to get married again. And even if he could *I* couldn't marry him as my husband's still alive and our religion prevents us from getting divorced. So, Reginald and I help each other, sir, and spend a lot of time together."

"He is a very lucky man," Hardy remarked.

"It's an arrangement which suits us both," the nurse replied soberly. "The thing is, sir — he *hates* — he hates all kinds of promiscuity and casual infidelity. He *hates* it."

"So, he hates the Merryfield Community," Hardy murmured. "Isn't that what you are saying?"

"Magnificent," Cellini applauded. "Wonderful, John!" And he felt nothing like so tired as he had a few minutes ago.

The nurse who had an arrangement with Reginald Atkinson, the nurse who was at once frightened and bold at the same time, moved away from the bed where Mary Wilberforce still lay; but lay now with her eyes closed, breathing much more easily. It was as if the voices had lulled her off to natural sleep. Cars moved and people walked outside but the first aid room seemed to be under some kind of benevolent protection.

"Yes," the nurse said. "He regards it as a den of iniquity. He's always said that sooner or later it would be shown up for what it is, and today, well, I think it's one of the reasons for his collapse, sir. I happened to be with him this morning when he was told what had happened, and when you telephoned to say you were coming. And if I may say so, sir, he said he was very glad you were and hoped you could take over the investigation, *he* couldn't trust himself to be objective. And then later apparently Dr. Cellini—" she turned towards Cellini, who looked startled at being brought into the conversation, "talked about it being a kind of visitation of the devil, well that *really* set him off, sir. He said it was a bloody sight more likely to be the hand of God, if there is a God—I'm quoting him, sir—and that all psychiatrists were—" she broke off, swallowed something and then added lamely: "unreliable, sir."

"I am sure you mean he called me a quack," Cellini remarked urbanely. "A large number of people do. If I may say so, we owe you a great deal, Nurse. You have helped us to understand many things which were baffling. Don't you agree, John?"

"Fully." Hardy smiled at the nurse, held the smile for some seconds then turned to Mary, who looked so serene; so young; and so attractive. It was hard to believe that such a short time ago she had been near death; and that less than twenty-four hours ago she had lost the man whom she and her world regarded as her husband. "Now you may be able to help us again, Nurse."

"With this young woman?"

"Yes."

"I don't think there's much doubt what to do with her," the nurse said. "Just round the corner there is a private guest house where we often send girls who have problems. Unless they've actually been arrested it's much better to send them to a place that looks like home, than to a cell. And a guest house can be guarded if necessary. I don't think she'll be round for two or three hours yet, anyhow," the nurse added. "She was in a terribly low state. May I ask what trouble she was in?"

Hardy told her.

"Oh, my goodness," the nurse exclaimed, and

she had never looked more human. "It's almost as if you're right, Dr. Cellini, and it *is* the work of the devil."

"It will be the work of an angel of mercy if you will arrange for her to go to the guest house," Cellini replied.

"Under guard," urged Hardy with a grim smile. "I should hate any devil, human or not, to get at her while she's under our protection! I must go and see the officer in charge. Manny, would you like to go home? I doubt if anything more will happen tonight, and in the morning—"

"You can't get rid of me as easily as that," Cellini protested. "But it must be getting late, and I could do with a wash and some supper. Do you think that can be arranged, Nurse?"

"There's a cloakroom here where you can wash and a lovely little café only just round the corner," the nurse answered. "The food's much better than anything you could get in the canteen here."

"You are very kind," Cellini said, and he went into the cloakroom while Hardy went upstairs and Mary Wilberforce "slept" and he wondered how Carol Smith was and whether the police car driver had been hurt, and just what was going on in the Merryfield Community and why.

And he wondered who had killed Wilberforce.

An hour later, he sat up in Atkinson's office with Hardy, eating sandwiches which had after all been sent up from the canteen. Hardy had a great deal to report, and did so while eating and drinking. He looked brisk and businesslike, and at half-past nine, showed no signs of stress after the long day.

The driver of the police car had been bruised, but not badly.

The car had a buckled wheel and wing but was not seriously damaged.

Mary Wilberforce was in the guest house, under guard.

Carol Smith was still in the small private ward at the hospital, but had said nothing more. She had dozed on and off during the day.

Two men and two women from the Merryfield Community had come to see the girls and to offer help but had not insisted on staying when the police had assured them there was no need.

The latest reports from Scobie at the Community were negative; no one admitted having seen or heard anyone leave the Community during the relevant hours.

No further clues had been found at the place where the murder had been committed.

The evening newspapers in London had treated the story warily, not giving it too much space, but the Press was becoming more insistent, and he, Hardy, had issued another statement giving the simple facts and stating that neither girl was under charge or even suspicion but was being kept under close observation because each might have seen the killer.

A police surgeon who had been treating Atkinson had stated that Atkinson should really have been retired at least a year ago, on the grounds of ill health.

Scobie, who had returned from Merryfield after dark, and had now gone home, had admitted to Hardy that he had really been trying to alert Hardy to Atkinson's health condition. "The situation had difficulty, sir, but my main concerns were that Mr. Atkinson should be relieved from working pressure and that the general efficiency of the division should not be impaired."

And finally:

"I talked to Woman Police Constable Bessington," he said, "and she is taking Carol Smith from the hospital and to her flat. I gathered from you that you think this could be very useful."

"She might get that girl to talk," Manny Cellini observed, and with a positively seraphic smile he went on: "I am sure you feel as I do that one or the other of the girls *can* answer all the questions, John. That one or both, and probably both, have so far told you only half the truth."

Hardy cut off a piece of crumbly red Cheshire cheese, and replied: "That could be why I've kept them away from Merryfield, couldn't it? And it may be why every road from Merryfield, every section of the boundaries of the Commu-

nity, is being closely watched." A smile shone
deep in Hardy's eyes. "It could also be why I've
arranged for an electronic contact system: no
one can get away from Merryfield without being
seen or without touching a wire which will ring
an alarm here at the station." As he saw Cellini's
expression, he chuckled with deep enjoyment.
"Did you really think I was so overcome by the
atmosphere up there that I forgot to do the essential things?" he asked.

"No," replied Cellini. "I simply had not
realised how many things were essential." He
gave a *tch-tch-tch-tch* of impatience with himself.
"No doubt the day will dawn when I realise that
my preoccupation with the psychological and the
emotional is really such a small part of the necessary preoccupations with daily living," he went
on. "I seek to know why a man or woman does
what is done; even what they are likely to be
driven to do by the intensity of their own feeling
for good and evil.

"Good and evil," he repeated, drawing a deep
breath. "John—"

"I know exactly what you are going to tell me,"
Hardy interrupted. "That given the right pres-
sures and emotions, good can turn into evil as
love can turn into hate? I'm thinking about the
bundle of nerves and psychoses which make up
Joshua Smith, too. Now!" Hardy got up from
the small table at which they had been eating.
"Everything is under control. I will stake my rep-

utation that nothing will go wrong with our precautions. Both girls should be much more themselves in the morning. You can go home to Felisa
and have a good night's sleep. I have to go to the
Yard and then on to Bull, who lives close by. I
don't think I told you that after I began to explain on the telephone, John Bull simply said
'come to my home.' So I'm going."

"I confess that I would not want to be up and
active much longer. If you could arrange for a
taxi—"

"Nonsense! I'll fix a police car."

"I meant, George's taxi," Cellini said, mildly.

Hardy stared at him; and then again burst into
a chuckle. Soon a call was going for "George"
who knew what to do with Atkinson, and Hardy
was saying to Cellini:

"If you stayed home and did nothing more,
what you've done would still be invaluable,
Manny. If we'd just blundered into Merryfield
without warning heaven knows what a mess we'd
be in."

"Our real anxiety is what kind of a mess
Merryfield is in," Cellini retorted.

15

Still Night

"JOHN," SAID COMMANDER BULL to Chief Detective Superintendent Hardy, "what's going on?"

"John," said Hardy to the Commander of the Criminal Investigation Department, "it looks to me as if these people at Merryfield Community have tried to turn their backs on life while keeping one foot in the outside world, but life has jumped in ahead of them."

"Very graphic," remarked Bull, stretching out his long lean legs from his deep armchair in a living-room-cum-study in his London house, "but it doesn't tell me much." He sniffed appreciatively at the bouquet of the brandy cupped in his hands and leaned his head against the high back of the winged armchair. "Are you telling me that it looks as if this man Wilberforce played around with so many women and girls that someone got plain jealous and strangled him?"

"I'm not sure it's as simple as that," replied Hardy.

"Then what?"

"I think I wish Cellini were here. He can make some things more convincing."

"I need facts to be convinced, not Manny's ifs and buts and perhaps," retorted Bull. But he smiled; he really was a most handsome and strong-looking man. "Not that I've anything against Manny, and taken by and large I think you were right to give him his head as you did."

"I did hold the reins," Hardy remarked; and he levelled his gaze at his superior and lowered his nose to the big bowl-shaped brandy glass. Nothing could have been more welcome, soothing, curiously refreshing. He sniffed slowly and appreciatively but did not once shift his gaze.

"I'm sure you did," said Bull. "I'm also sure that Manny can slip the reins whenever he's in the mood and can square it with that remarkable sense of right and wrong of his. *Is* he still working for Joshua Smith?"

"I avoided putting the question to him," Hardy answered.

"Why?"

"Because at this moment I think he thinks that our interests and Smith's are identical, and I don't want a conflict on a technicality. You must know as well as I do that if it appears to Manny that our interests conflict, he'll tell us so, and either withdraw from us or from Smith. And surely you know without it being put into words that his chief purpose was to gain time."

"For what?"

"The Community."

"I wondered if you'd seen that," Bull said, drily.

"John," said Hardy, drawing his face away from the brandy and lowering his glass so that he held it cupped in both hands, on his lap, "Manny Cellini expected a conflict between Smith and *someone*. Whether he knew it was Ryall, I don't know, but he was fully aware that a crisis was in the offing."

"So was Smith, or he wouldn't have sent for Manny."

"I knew it," said Hardy, as if resignedly. "There you are a step ahead of me all the time."

"That's not always difficult," retorted Bull. "What were you going to say?"

"The crisis might be over a challenge for the leadership," Hardy said. "It's a long way from being a great big happy family at Merryfield. Or it might be over Wilberforce the Fornicator. Or it might be because someone else is breaking all their rules. Whatever the reason there's a lot of tension and conflict and—" he raised his glass

again, sniffed, and looking at Bull over the edge,
went on: "talk of the devil."

"I wondered when you would get to that," Bull
said. He leaned forward and took a cigar from
an ashtray at his side, lit it, then, waiting until his
head was enveloped in blue-grey smoke and the
air filled with a pungent but pleasing aroma,
went on: "Does Cellini take it seriously? Horns
and cloven hoof and all, I mean?"

"I would never like to swear what Manny
Cellini thinks or believes but I would doubt
whether he's going round Merryfield looking in
the grass for prints of the cloven hoof," answered Hardy. "If he saw one the probability is
that he would plump for cow. But he takes Carol
Smith's fear of the devil seriously. Very
seriously."

"So does Atkinson," said Bull quietly.

"What?" Hardy was so surprised that he
started up and the brandy lapped to the rim of
the glass.

"It's a fact," Bull said soberly.

"But this morning—"

"He was enraged about it, you told me," Bull
said quietly.

"He was more than enraged. He was almost
berserk. At one time I thought he was going to
manhandle our Manny. And if he could have
done so he would most certainly have fired Police Constable Bessington on the spot." Hardy
placed his glass on a table which touched the arm

of the chair, and went on more heavily: "But you don't know about Atkinson, do you?"

"I know he's not a fit man," replied Bull. "In fact that's one of the things I wanted—" He broke off. "But I'm interrupting. What's new about him?"

Hardy told him what had happened at the Halling police station; enough of the relationship with the nurse to allow the Commander to read between the lines of the fat superintendent's personal life, and of the certainty that Atkinson would be off duty for several days at least. Bull asked one or two searching questions, about how widely known this situation was at Halling Division. They were sitting looking at each other, as if wondering who should speak next, when there was a ring at the front door bell. Bull started as violently as Hardy had done a few moments before, sprang up and hurried out of the room, saying over his shoulder:

"Who on earth can that be at this time of night? Gwen's in bed." His voice faded, his footsteps made hardly any sound, and when at last he spoke it was on a muted note, the quietness of which did not disguise his astonishment. "What the devil are you doing here?"

Dr. Cellini said in his quiet but carrying voice: "To talk of the devil, Commander. I do hope I've not missed John Hardy and that I'm not too late for you."

"No," Bull said. "Come in." A moment later he

ushered Cellini into the room, pushed up another of the huge winged chairs and offered
brandy. Hardy, on his feet, was looking down at
the older man as if he didn't know whether to be
pleased or sorry to see him.

"Brandy would be *just* right," said Cellini,
dropping into his chair with every appearance of
physical weakness; but his eyes were very bright.
He took the glass and inhaled. "Surely—surely a
very old Napoleon," he breathed ecstatically. "I
had no idea you were such a connoisseur, Commander. Thank you, thank you."

"I thought you'd gone home for an early
night," Hardy said accusingly.

"Yes, indeed, and so I had. But the best laid
schemes *do* sometimes go awry, you know. I had
not been home for more than five minutes when
Elizabeth, from the Community, telephoned me.
She was in a state of controlled hysteria. She said
that she and most of the women at Merryfield
are terrified of Ryall. That although some of the
men and a few of the women like him, for the
most part he fills them with terror.

"And tonight—" Cellini paused, to inhale and
to sip, and then went on: "Tonight, since darkness fell, the Community has been full of strange
noises and of shadowy figures although the men
have found no one. I want to know whether any
of your people are about the grounds, John. If
they are not, then who is causing this virtual
reign of terror?"

Hardy said into the telephone, two minutes later: "Are you absolutely sure?"

"Positive sir," the inspector-in-charge on night duty said. "None of our men has stepped over the electronic control system. Do you want us to?"

"Not yet. Stand by," Hardy ordered. "Is anyone at Pucklebury Ring?"

"Two men, sir, keeping a general eye on things."

"Thank you," Hardy said. "Just keep the closest watch. Are there enough of our chaps surrounding Merryfield to pick up half-a-dozen men if they should come away from the place?"

"Plenty, sir."

"Good. Tell them to be on their toes."

He rang off on the man's "I will, sir," and reported to Bull and Cellini.

"None of our chaps is actually inside, and no one's gone in as far as they know."

"Noises," Cellini said.

"Someone could be using the loudspeaker system," Hardy remarked.

"Yes, but—" began Cellini.

"What seems to matter most is whether we ought to send someone inside to find out what's happening," Bull interrupted. "It looks to me as if someone is trying to throw a scare into all the members."

"Trying!" ejaculated Cellini, but he was calm enough to glance at his watch. It was exactly midnight. "Gentlemen," he went on, "this situation has troubled me more than anything else. I know it could be a matter of high tension, of a kind of nervous breakdown, but the woman Elizabeth did not strike me as the kind whose nerves would crack easily. I came here for two reasons," he added. "I thought it would be much more effective if I came in person instead of telephoning; and also because I arranged for Elizabeth to telephone here at midnight. I promised her I would ask you to send police into the grounds if the noises did not cease. It is now one minute past twelve. I—"

The telephone bell rang, and all three stared at the grey-coloured instrument on the table by John Bull's side. Quickly but deliberately he took off the receiver. All of them could hear the *bip-bip-bip-bip* of a call from a prepayment call box. *Bip-bip-bip-bip* it went, and Bull said: "Hallo," and after a pause, more loudly: "*Hallo*. Do you want Dr. Cellini? . . . *Bip-bip-bip-bip* . . . *Hallo*. Are you there? *Hallo!*" Bull roared, then sprang urgently to his feet.

Elizabeth stood at the door of her chalet, close to Joshua Smith's home in the administration building. Only the stars gave light; the moon that had been shining earlier had faded. The outline of trees and of other houses showed against the stars. In one window, across the clearing, there was light: a square of yellow.

There was no sound and no wind and the stillness seemed absolute.

She closed the door with infinite care and stepped onto the grass. Not far away, by the main Community buildings, were two telephone kiosks, the only two at Merryfield. No light showed at them.

She went nearer, heart thumping.

Had she been imagining things, earlier? Was she so afraid that her mind and her heart played tricks? Those noises—a groaning—had surely been real. And the shadows too. Now she saw darkness and not even her own shadow loomed. No tree-limb creaked. No wind stirred.

Suddenly, in front of her, a figure moved.

She did not know whether it was man or woman—or even beast. It moved upright on two feet; hurrying. She caught her breath. She did not see it turn, did not know whether she had been noticed. All she knew was that it crossed her path. Heart thumping wildly, she started off again. Now she could make out the shape of the telephone kiosks. How she wished they were lighted! She was only forty yards away and looking in all directions, even trying to look behind her.

She heard sounds; thudding, as of running footsteps.

"Oh, God!" she gasped. "Oh, God!" and she spun round.

No one was near, but close to one of the

houses there was a moving shape, as of a man or
woman running. Elizabeth could not move, just
stared and stared until the figure disappeared
and she could not be sure whether she had seen
it in reality or in her mind. At last, hands
clenched, heart beating with sickening thumps,
she turned towards the kiosks again and took
some faltering steps. She made ten yards or so,
hearing nothing, and seeing nothing and then
across the stillness and the silence, came a different sound.

A sighing.

A hissing.

A sighing *hiss-siss hiss-siss* of sound which, faint
at first, became louder and louder until it
seemed enough to deafen her. She looked round
wildly but there was no one in sight, only the
trees and the clearing and the buildings and the
stars. At last she was able to bring herself to go
on again. She had to talk to Cellini. *She had to talk
to Cellini.* He was her one contact with familiar
sanity in the outside world and she was sure he
wanted to help.

She reached the nearer kiosk and stepped inside; and a light came on.

She placed a coin in the slot and began to dial,
reading the number she had written down on a
slip of paper which she took from the pocket of
her robe.

The sighing and the hissing was going on and
on.

She heard first the *brr-brr-brr-brr* and very soon the *bip-bip-bip-bip-bip* which told her that someone at the other end had answered. Now she had to press the coin in and there would surely be Cellini. A man was saying in a deep voice:

"*Hallo . . . Hallo . . .*"

She pressed the coin with her forefinger. It stuck. She pressed again and it still stuck while the man at the other end called: "*Hallo.* Do you want Dr. Cellini?" How she wanted him, how desperately she wished that he hadn't gone away.

Then, a shadow fell upon her, as the coin at last dropped into the box.

She looked up and saw a man over whose face was drawn a cowl which hid all his features but had wide slits for the eyes. She stood in absolute terror as he pulled open the door. His hands, gloved hands, moved towards her. She dropped the telephone and it clattered and clanged and then swung by its cord. The hands were rising towards her throat. She tried to scream but could not. Cramped in this tiny box she could only move one way: forward. Suddenly, propelled by desperation, she tried to thrust her way forward striking at his hands, but it was like striking iron bars. He did not speak. The sighing, hissing sound came very clearly. The kiosk echoed to a man's voice booming: "*Hallo!* Are you there? *Hallo!* She felt the hands touch her throat. She knew how Wilberforce had died. She felt the pressure of thumbs and fingers. She kicked but all to no avail. She tried to knee the man who was attacking her, in the groin, but he was standing in such a way that she could only strike the strong muscles in his thigh.

She could just make out the sheen in his eyes as he pressed and pressed, and she not only felt pain at her neck and in her head and pressure at the back of her eyes, but she could not breathe.

16

Double for P.C. Dimitry

POLICE CONSTABLE DIMITRY relived the night before as he stood or moved about the road just
outside the main entrance to Merryfield Community. It was a beautifully clear night, cool but
not cold; about the same as last night, he re-
called. He had been walking along on his beat,
on the lookout for anything; couples in the backs
of cars for instance. Cars without rear lights, or
even a man coming furtively out of a gateway.
There might be a window open where it should
be closed . . .

Suddenly, in his mind, he heard the scream.

He did not think he would ever forget the way
it had pierced silence; or the way he had at first

seemed to go cold, and his muscles to shrink, and then how he had exploded into action.

No, he would never forget it.

He was at that point in his thinking, and about to go over the run in his mind, and next the moment when he had found the girl and the way he had jumped to the conclusion that the only chance for her was the kiss of life, when his radio squawked with the same suddenness as the scream had come last night. He saw another man perhaps fifty yards away snatch at his receiver too, and realised that everyone here was being called. It was probably a routine check.

He heard a man with an excited voice say: "Get into Merryfield, quick! There's trouble by the telephone kiosk, *get there quick.*"

"My God," breathed Dimitry.

He had been in the Community grounds, earlier, and he knew the relative position of the entrance, the road and the telephone kiosks. And—quite as quickly as in his reliving of yesterday's events—he went into action. If he followed that winding road it would take an age, but if he could find a gap in the hedge he could make a bee-line for the buildings and the kiosks; being caught in electronic beams no longer mattered. Being on the far side of the road from the hedge he could see the outline, and spotted a place where it was much lower than along most of its length; either a bush had been cleared or one had died. On the instant, he decided not to try to

orce his way through anywhere but to make a
unning jump; with luck he might just clear the
op.

He judged the distance, took a sideways run
nd leapt, tucking his legs beneath him, and had
ime to hope that it wouldn't be too rough where
ıe landed. He saw a small tree, swung his body,
rashed through the outer branches and landed
ıgainst the slender trunk, which bent but did not
ɔreak. He straightened up, and began to run.
He was in an orchard, where the young trees
vere widely spaced so he had little difficulty in
ᴄarving a path through them. He could not yet
ᴄee the outline of the buildings but did see a yel-
ow square of light, obviously a window.

A car started up in the road: a police car. He
vould beat it with ease!

He drew out his torch and carried it in his left
ıand, the beam swinging wildly. The engine
ᴄoared. A police whistle blew. Another car en-
ᴄine started up. Two more lighted squares leapt
ınto the darkness. He ran as fast—faster—than
ıe had the previous night, for the ground was
ᴄore even. Soon he was on one of the great
ᴄawns which swept towards the Community
ɔuildings. Another light leapt on. The car en-
ᴄines sounded very loud as he saw the light of a
ᴄiosk—and a man who was leaving it; and he
hought he saw a woman's head, inside.

He saw the cowl-like hood; saw the man run;
ᴄhen lost him in dark shadows; but the kiosk

light stayed on. He could judge the gene
rection in which the man was going and
cut him off, but whoever was still in the k
and there must be someone or the light
have gone out—might be in urgent need o
He was running very easily now, sure th
would be well ahead of the other police bu
when the headlights of a car appeared, m
they had last night. They shone on the kio
flected from its windows, and suddenly he
no doubt at all.

A woman was leaning over the telephon
the bracket on which it stood, head lollin
strange way. He could only see her head, p
her face and one shoulder. The beam o
headlight changed direction but he did no
it any more, his own torch would give
enough. He glanced towards the area cover
the beam and caught a glimpse of the cowle
ure, running; and beyond, several of th
tages. The men in the car might get the fu
He, Dimitry, had to concentrate on the w
in the kiosk.

He reached it and pulled the door ope
did not recognise her but could see that sh
a middle-aged and full-bodied woman. Th
the light was fairly good in the kiosk, this w
place to attempt a resuscitation. He hes
only for a moment before bending down
ting his arms about the woman's waist and
dragging, half-lifting her. Now the headlig

another car shone fully on to them both, and as he stretched her out on to the grass the car stopped and a man hurried from it.

"She all right?" he called.

"Don't know!" grunted Dimitry. "She's nearly had it."

"Any chance?"

"She can't have been out long, so there must be."

"Well," the other man said, "you're the expert."

Dimitry, only half-believing that this could have happened to him on successive nights, went down on his knees and began the kiss of life. The other man began to feel for her waist and any constriction and Dimitry heard him say in a startled voice: "She's as cold as ice."

"*In—out.*" Dimitry was breathing into the woman's mouth. "*In—out.*"

By that time, Cellini and Bull were getting into Hardy's car, and the detective sergeant driver was starting the engine. They were in touch with *Information* at the Yard and *Information* was passing on news as it arrived from Halling. So far, only one positive fact was established: that a woman had been attacked. That could hardly be called news, for nothing else could have explained what had happened at the telephone. Cellini was sitting in a corner, staring out of the window, Hardy next to him, Bull next to the driver. Hardy held the walkie-talkie, which was built into the back of the front passenger seat.

"You there, sir?" The voice of the man from *Information* sounded clearly in the car.

"Hardy speaking."

"They say that a cowled or hooded figure attacked the woman."

"Have they caught him yet?"

"No, sir."

"Any chance he could have got through the cordon?" Bull demanded in a penetrating whisper.

Information picked that up. "I'll find out, sir."

"Any word of the woman?" asked Hardy.

"One of our men is trying to revive her, sir."

"I want to know the moment there's news."

"I won't break contact with you, sir."

Hardy grunted, placed the mouthpiece against his chest, and peered forward at Bull, twisted round in his seat. The car was gathering speed along Bayswater Road and would soon swing off into Hyde Park, since Halling lay beyond the East End, towards the east.

"What's next?" Bull asked.

"I'd like to draft a lot more men into Merryfield and have every man, woman and child there questioned tonight."

"Then do it," Bull authorised.

"Information!" Hardy called with both restrained impatience and excitement in his voice, "We want a hundred men in Halling within the next hour, and a house-to-house questioning in

the Merryfield Community. Who is on duty in my office?"

"Chief Inspector Drewitt, sir."

"Tell him to organise this without losing a moment," Hardy ordered. "He can call me in the car or at Halling."

"It shall be done, sir."

"Thank you. Can you get me whoever is in charge at Halling?"

"Mr. Scobie's just been on the line, sir. You may find the line a bit noisy but I could get him for you."

"Then do. I'll hold on." Hardy put the mouthpiece against his chest again, and for the first time looked out of the window. In a way this wasn't unlike Merryfield, for they were now in Hyde Park and the headlights blazed startlingly on trees and bushes. Cellini now sat with his chin on his chest, as if he were dozing. Hardy saw Bull beating a tattoo on the dashboard with the fingers of his right hand.

There were some squeaky atmospherics before a man said:

"Scobie here, sir."

"Where are you?" asked Hardy.

"At Merryfield—I'd gone to have a final check that the place was properly covered."

"Is it?" demanded Hardy.

Scobie said: "There's a possibility that someone escaped at the place where our men went in, sir, but it's not likely."

"But possible?" insisted Hardy.

"Yes, sir, but the man seen running awa[y]
in the north-east corner where our guard v[as]
affected," Scobie told him. "The men [I]
moved in were all from the main entrance, i[n]
south-west, so there's a good chance he's s[till in]
the Community."

"I want him," Hardy growled.

"Believe me, sir, so do I!"

Hardy said: "Was the victim the woma[n I]
saw this afternoon, Elizabeth?"

"Yes, sir."

"How—" Hardy choked. "How is she?"

"Well," Scobie began in a voice which c[ould]
have meant anything, "it rather looks [as if]
Dimitry has done it again, sir."

Hardy, puzzled, said: "Done what ag[ain?]
And then he realised who Dimitry was and [what]
this meant and the tone of his voice chang[ed to]
one of relief and even excitement. "You m[ean]
she's alive?"

"Yes, and, as far as I can judge, out of [dan]ger," Scobie said. "A doctor's on his way [now]
and we should have his report by the time [you]
get here."

"Good," Hardy said with deep satisfac[tion.]
"Has *Information* told you that I've ordere[d an]other hundred men into the Merryfield C[om]munity, and I want a house-to-house call to[day]
with the most rigorous questioning. If the[y offer]
any opposition to it—but never mind, I'[ll]

there before serious oposition can form. Is there any word from the guest house or from Woman Police Constable Bessington?"

"I've just had a report from the men who have both places under surveillance," Scobie replied, "and all's quiet. No alarms of any kind."

"Make sure it stays that way," Hardy said, and rang off.

Cellini raised his head at last and shifted his position. He listened intently to Hardy reporting to Bull, and when Hardy had finished, he said apologetically:

"John, I know how irritating it can be to be re-minded of something by a third party but should you check whether Joshua Smith and Samuel Ryall have been in their rooms all the evening? I know it may sound ridiculous to suspect Smith of attacking Elizabeth but if we can be sure of any-thing it is that a kind of devil *is* loose, and the only place I expect to find the devil is in a man."

Hardy grunted.

"If I know Scobie he made a bee-line for both men," he said. "But I'll check." He called *Information* again and sent a message through to Scobie; and almost at once a reply came:

"Both Smith and Ryall are asleep in their beds, sir."

"Asleep?" asked Cellini.

"Both of them."

"Remarkable!"

"What's remarkable?" Bull growled.

"That after such a disturbance and the accompanying noise they should be asleep."

"People do sleep like logs," Bull grunted.

"I do myself," admitted Hardy. "I was afraid they might have had their throats cut."

"Or been strangled," Bull said.

"Asleep," said Cellini, and he sighed a deep sigh. "How long will it take us to get there?"

"Half an hour, I suppose," Hardy said.

"Twenty minutes when there's no traffic, sir," said the driver.

"Why?" demanded Bull.

"I'd like to know what made those two men sleep like logs," Cellini said.

"Are you saying they might have been drugged?"

"Yes," Cellini said. "Yes, indeed I am."

"We can make a start on finding that out before we get there," Hardy said. "Who do you think would—" He broke off.

"Another question first," Bull said.

"What's that, sir?" Hardy asked, very formal with the driver and Cellini present.

"How long have they been asleep?"

"Another," murmured Cellini.

Hardy said in a tone of exasperation: "We may as well have them all while we're about it."

"Yes," said Cellini, and touched the back of his friend's hand. "How long *will* they sleep?"

Hardy exclaimed: "My God!" He called *Information* in a sharp voice, and became almost shrill when he wasn't answered at once. "Hallo, *Information. Infor*—Oh, I want Halling again, urgently."

"Very good, sir. Does it matter who?"

"Preferably Mr. Scobie, but anyone in authority will do."

"Just a moment, sir."

They were going up a long hill now, and the streetlamps made a tunnel of pale light. A few cars came towards them but none passed and none was likely to. The driver had caught the sense of urgency which drove the others. He took the right fork at the top of the hill, past a public house. A uniformed policeman stepped out of a gateway and stood watching them.

"But *who?*" demanded Bull. "Who would want them dead?"

"Now that *is* a question," Cellini said. "May I ask another?" He looked apologetically at Hardy, who simply grunted. "Why attack Elizabeth?"

"She was trying to get help," Hardy said sharply.

"For whom?"

"For the whole Community. She was terrified."

"For whom is a very good question," remarked Cellini, his gentleness contrasting with Hardy's harsh voice. Hardy was obviously seething with suppressed tension; in a mood to blame himself for anything or everything that went wrong.

"Herself? Joshua? The Community? It is a
thing she is alive and can speak. John—"

"Mr. Scobie is just coming on the line, sir
formation said, and added as if he simply
not keep it to himself: "There's more troul
some kind out there. They ought to call
place Merry Hell, not Merryfield. I—here i
Scobie, sir."

The atmospherics sounded again, and it i
have been worsened by the heavy breathi
the man who had been hurrying. It seem
long time before Scobie actually spoke, and
before he uttered a word all the men in th
were filled with foreboding.

Then Scobie said: "It's touch and go with
Joshua Smith and the man Ryall, sir. Bot
parently took or were given some kind of
last night. The only thing we know is tha
tablets contained morphia. An ambulance
its way to collect them and the hospital is s
ing by."

17

Near Unto Death

EVERY WORD WAS clearly audible in the car; every word made its own sharp impact. Each of the men was looking down at the instrument in Hardy's hand. There was a metallic tremor whenever they went over a slight bump in the road. After Scobie's "and the hospital is standing by," there was stillness and quiet within the car. Then Hardy broke it with a restrained:

"Thank you, Inspector. Double the precautions at the guest house and at W.P.C. Bessington's home."

"I will at once, sir."

"And keep in touch," Hardy ordered. "I suppose—" He broke off and placed the receiver slowly on its hook, rubbed his chin and muttered as if to himself: "If they'd found anybody he'd have said so." In sudden exasperation he turned to Cellini: "Did you expect an upheaval like this?"

"It was the very danger I was consulted to avoid," Cellini answered, and he added in a remote and humble way: "A task in which I failed woefully."

The car sped on. Headlights of cars approaching flashed by. They were near Halling now and it was surprising how many houses had lighted windows. But in most of those they passed the people were sleeping and the night was hushed. In some there would be the anxiety caused by illness and by human emotional conflict; in some, fear of death and in others the grief caused by it. Everyone was in his own little world, and just ahead was the world which Joshua Smith had tried to build, welding a group of people together.

Yet each was his self: each lived in his own world, each had his own loves and hates and fears.

As if speaking out of a reverie, Bull said: "Well, *we* mustn't fail. We want that man."

"Manny," Hardy began, and stopped, but looked intently, demandingly at Cellini.

"What do you wish to ask me?" Cellini enquired.

"Have you any idea who has done this?"

"Good God!" exclaimed Bull, "you wouldn't keep anything back from us, would you?"

"I might keep guesses from you," Cellini said. "But in such a situation as this, I would never withhold facts. No, John, I do not know who has done these evil things."

"Who's your guess?" demanded Bull, twisting round in his seat.

"I do not think I am yet in a position to make a guess," replied Cellini.

"Did Joshua Smith ever give a hint?"

"No. As I have already told John, he asked me to try to help him find out who was set on destroying the contentment and the smooth running of the Community. He knew that Lionel Wilberforce was behaving—I use his word—like a lecher. He knew others were being unfaithful; again I quote him. He knew that some of the women were frightened to go out on their own at night, a situation which had never existed before. Everything he had hoped for and planned was in danger of destruction and he wanted me to help find the cause. Was it a rival for his position as Patriarch? Was it simply that the seeds of failure were within the experiment itself? Could human beings live in harmony only for a short time before dissension set in and the well-known and tried human weaknesses of lust and greed and pride and vanity and longing for power, latent in the hearts of men, took over once again?

"Or—" Cellini paused, for the car swung
round a corner and threw him against Hardy.
The driver murmered: "Sorry sir, I was listening
to you too intently." Neither of the others spoke.
The headlights shone on a sign which read: *The
London Borough of Halling*. They took the right
fork just beyond this towards the Community.
They were very close now to the place where
there had been so much hope destroyed by hate
or fear.

Cellini was saying: "Or, Joshua Smith wanted
to know, *is* there an all-pervading evil spirit. A
devil. *The* devil." When no one spoke he went
on: "You see, he had rejected the conventional
concept of God. He had replaced it by the concept of good—human good and universal good.
He believed that this arose out of the human
heart and mind and spirit. But now that everything he had built was crashing about his head
he began to torment himself by wondering
whether he was not suffering from the vengeance of God, visited upon him by the devil."

The word "devil" came up with extra force,
because the driver touched his brake too
sharply; as they turned a corner a man stood
flashing a light at them, and they drew level with
a sign which read: *Police*. So they were at the
Community, where the ugly world of murder
and attempted murder had taken over from a
striving for goodness.

The driver said "I've Commander Bull and Super—"

A torchlight shone on their faces, an invisible man said "Okay, sir," and the car started on again, passing several other men before reaching the main entrance to Merryfield. Now a light from the grounds swayed up and down, showing an approaching car, and a policeman put out a commanding arm, barring their way. Almost at once an ambulance turned out of Merryfield and turned in the other direction. The arm waved them on. Bull wound down his window and called:

"Is Mr. Scobie here?"

"Up at the centre, sir."

Bull nodded. The driver went very slowly along the curving road. Lights showed in dozens of places. Two men with Alsatian dogs appeared on the verge, the eyes of the dogs glistening. The tires crunched on the gravel, as the driver went even more slowly.

It was Bull who asked, abruptly:

"What did you tell Smith?"

Cellini said, slowly: "That I would try to help."

"Didn't you tell him that talk of the devil was all my eye?"

"No," said Cellini. "No, I did not. For how can I, how can *any* man be sure of that?"

"So you let him think—"

"No!" interrupted Cellini sharply. "I did not

let him think anything; he thought for himself. I told him that in all my experience the devil, if he existed, lived in the hearts and minds of men and acted through men, not by evil manifestation from unknown sources. But whether the devil *is* man or whether he works through man or whether he is a figment in the mind of man who longs for an excuse for his own wickedness, I do not know." He sat back in his seat, but before either of the others spoke the car drew up in a clearing where several other cars were parked and a dozen men were congregated. "I would like your permission, John, to go and talk to Mary Wilberforce and to Carol Smith," he went on. "They still might know more than anyone else about this, and Carol might even have talked to the remarkable Police Constable Bessington."

Hardy said: "You will tell us anything they say, won't you?"

"Of course."

"Then I've no objection."

"It might even help, and God knows we need some help," Bull growled, as the car stopped and men moved from either side to open the doors. Now it was possible to see exactly what was going on. The police had taken over the Meeting House, by the telephones. The double doors stood open and the lights were on. Tables had been drawn up, and chairs in front of them. Several members of the Community were sitting opposite police officers who were asking them set questions. More members of the Community were coming down from the houses, in groups escorted by policemen.

Scobie came hurrying from one of these groups.

"Sorry I wasn't here to meet you," he said, briskly. "*Very* glad to see you, gentlemen." Whether that was true or not, he made it sound convincing.

"Any change in the two men?" asked Hardy.

"Not when they left here five minutes ago, sir."

"Any idea what poison they took?"

"One of the narcotics, sir; the pupils of the eyes were pin-points."

"Any sign of the man we're after?"

"No, sir," Scobie said, "none at all. About eighty extra men have been drafted in and I thought it best to bring the members here for questioning and have each house and property searched in their absence. The other way could have taken much too long."

"Yes," Hardy said. "Did you brief the new men?"

"Just to search for a mask or a hood or a dunce's cap, anything which the man who attacked Elizabeth might have worn. Our men here are doing all the questioning and I'm checking after each interrogation." When none of the others spoke, Scobie went on: "We need to search the grounds at dawn, sir. With luck, if it's someone from outside, he's still hiding here. But he *could* have got away."

"Did you double the guard on the two girls?" demanded Bull.

"I made that the first job after talking to Mr. Hardy, sir. If it was someone from outside and if he did attack the woman and poison the men, then obviously the girls might be next on his list. But I don't care who tries, sir, no one will get past our men. I've just been up to check. Every door and window is being watched, the roofs are, too; it simply isn't possible for anyone to force a way into the guest house or into Police Constable Bessington's flat without being seen. We've even brought George's taxi in for extra help if we need it."

"Good," grunted Bull.

"I hope someone will give me safe conduct," Cellini said, diffidently. "I should hate to be taken for a would-be attacker."

"No fear of that sir," said Scobie, taking him literally. "I did wonder if you would want to see them, and I've a man on standby to take you wherever you want to go. P.C. Dimitry," he added, with a smile.

"*The* Dimitry?" exclaimed Bull, on the instant.

"The only one we've got on the strength," Scobie replied.

Police Constable Dimitry, standing nearby,

heard his name mentioned and then heard the Commander himself exclaim: "*The* Dimitry?" It was, for him, the supreme accolade. He was hardly able to speak when Bull and Hardy moved towards him, and Bull said: "Very nice work, Dimitry," and Hardy said: "It's lucky you know your first aid." Then Cellini came and added a gentle word of congratulation. Still in a daze, Dimitry made himself listen intently when Scobie said:

"Take Dr. Cellini wherever he wants to go, Constable."

"Yes, sir."

"You may be asked for your card of authority." Scobie went on. "All the men on duty at the two places you'll be visiting have been warned not to allow anyone to pass unless they are absolutely sure of their identity."

"I understand, sir."

"I don't exactly expect trouble but it could come," Scobie added. "Don't take the slightest chance."

"I won't, sir," promised P. C. Adam Dimitry, and he turned towards a waiting police car, a white one with a dark blue stripe over the top and down the sides.

Cellini got into the front passenger's seat and in a moment they were off, Hardy and Bull already talking to Scobie, as if he, Manny Cellini, was out of mind even before he was fully out of sight. Cellini stifled a yawn which was one of sheer tiredness, for it was now nearly two o'clock in the morning. He was glad that Dimitry kept his thoughts to himself; doubtless they were the kind of half daydream self-congratulatory thoughts which would possess such a man at such a time. Dimitry couldn't have made a better impression had he planned it for months. Nor, in his way, could Scobie. Cellini smiled a little at the recollection of the way Scobie was making sure he missed nothing and that the two senior policemen realised it. Who could blame him? Atkinson obviously wouldn't be in command at Halling for long, and Scobie must think he had a chance of getting the job.

Was that how Scotland Yard worked? wondered Cellini. Putting the right man in the right job because he *was* the right man? Or was it a question of seniority?

Dimitry asked: "Where would you like to go first, sir?"

"The guest house, I think."

"Very good, sir."

"Do you know how Mary Wilberforce is?"

"I telephoned twenty minutes or so ago and was told she had come round," said Dimitry, "but she hadn't talked except to ask for something to drink."

The guest house was one of a terrace of two-storey houses built of red brick, only a few hundred yards away from the police station. The glow from electric streetlamps housed in the old-

fashioned gas-lamp posts showed up the white-painted windows of *Number 11—Guest House.*
Two policemen moved about close to the front door, another stood opposite, a police car was pulled in nearby. The two policemen came forward as Dimitry slowed down and one of them put his head inside the car. Immediately, he said:

"Oh, it's you. Who's the gentleman with you?"

"Dr. Cellini," replied Dimitry.

"Oh, yes." Torchlight fell on Cellini's face. "It's all right to get out, sir, but have you some kind of identification?"

"Will my driving licence serve?" asked Cellini, taking out a bulky black wallet from his inside breast pocket. He had the driving licence in a special partition and took it out quickly. The bright centre spot of the light shone on it for a moment before the policeman handed it back.

"That's all right, sir. I'll tell my colleagues."

There were in fact two policemen inside, one just in the passage sitting at the foot of the stairs reading a paperback book which he put down hastily, another outside the door of the back room where Mary Wilberforce was. This man, big and bulky, tapped very softly on the door, and almost at once a woman in a nurse's uniform opened it. The bright hall-light shone on the face of the police nurse whom Cellini had seen at the first aid room.

"What is it?" she asked, in sharp undertones,

and then recognised Cellini. "Oh, it's you, Doctor."

"Is Mary asleep?" asked Cellini. "I'd like a few words with her."

"She's restless, really," the nurse said. "But you'll want to talk to her alone, I expect. While you're here, sir, I wonder if I could pop downstairs and get some hot milk and biscuits. I think the poor girl is hungry." With that disagreeable face and pleasant voice the nurse now added obvious concern for the patient.

"Of course," said Cellini. "But before you go—" he pulled the door to and asked in a voice which wouldn't travel inside the room: "Has she talked at all?"

"Only for the last few minutes," answered the nurse, as softly. "She both hates and loves this man of hers, and I don't think she yet fully realises that he's dead. She really *will* need looking after when she does realise it. Will you have to talk to her about her Lionel, Doctor?"

"Not very much, I hope," Cellini said. "You go and get that milk."

He went into the small, pleasantly furnished bedroom, with curtains and bedspread as well as chair-covers of brightly coloured, flowered linen, a small corner dressing-table with some bluebells on it in a tall vase, and a wardrobe in another corner. Every inch of space had been well utilised and the room looked much larger than it really was.

Mary was sitting back on pillows and a comfortable-looking bedrest. Books and magazines were on a small bedside table. The curtains were drawn and the room was perhaps overwarm and there was a strong scent either of perfume or cosmetics. These did not come from Mary, whose face had a fresh, scrubbed look, her wide-set eyes and rather high cheekbones giving her a startled, fawn-like expression. She looked no more than eighteen, partly because her hair was now drawn back from her forehead and tied in a pony tail. It showed the whiteness and the smoothness of her throat, and she wore a plain green nightdress with a shallow, rounded neckline which hinted at the depth of bosom.

Her eyes were such a beautiful clear grey.

And the fear in them was a hideous thing to see.

18

The Silent Fear

CELLINI WENT TO her, hands outstretched, hoping that she would take them and so feel some measure of the trust which she had shown when they had been in her Community home. Instead, she seemed to draw back against the walnut panel at the head of the bed and her eyes grew enormous as she looked at him.

"Hallo, Mary," he said. "I'm glad to see you're better."

She demanded: "What—what do you want?"

"I want to ask you a few questions," he said, his hands still extended. He looked so small and gentle—saintly—as he stood there and yet she looked upon him with fear. "If you can answer it might save a lot of time and anxiety later."

"I've told you all I can!" she cried, and drew still further back.

"Have you, Mary?" Cellini insisted. "Is that really true?"

"Yes!" she cried. "I didn't see anyone at Pucklebury Ring—except, except them! When it was over I ran away. It's so awful, every time I think about it, it seems to get worse. But I didn't see anything or anyone else." She put her hands up as if to fend him off and he was reminded of the way she had held them when he had first seen her; the same position as Joshua Smith's, as if she wanted to get her hands round someone's neck and squeeze.

As someone had squeezed her husband's until he had died.

And as someone had squeezed Elizabeth's tonight, until she had nearly died.

"Did you hear anyone screaming?" Cellini asked.

"*I* was screaming inside myself, it was just a nightmare. I ran and ran!"

If there had been other screaming, Cellini told himself, she would not have distinguished it from her own nightmare within herself. He did not think she was lying, and he wished he could help her. He backed away a foot or two and let his hands drop to his sides. He sat at the far end of the bed, so encouraging her to relax and sit more upright; but tension was still in her, and had the effect of making her look even younger than she had before.

And virginal.

It seemed absurd to think that she had borne two children.

"Mary," he said. "I want to help you."

"No one can help me!" she cried. "Lionel's dead and now I've got no one, no one at all."

"You have your friends at the Community, remember."

"Friends!" she echoed, with bitter scorn. "All they've done is talk behind my back, whispering and sniggering. Friends! I haven't any friends. I wish I'd never been born, oh, how I wish I'd never been born!"

"Mary," said Cellini, "do you think the Patriarch killed Lionel?"

For the first time since he had arrived he pierced the wall of fear and resistance, and saw her react as she really felt: astonished, horrified at the very thought. She sat up and leaned towards him, lips trembling, hands outstretched at last, but in pleading.

"Oh *no*. You can't believe *that*."

"I asked if you believed it," Cellini repeated.

"On *no*!" she repeated. "Joshua wouldn't, he's—he's too good, he's too kind. You—you don't think he did, do you? Please tell me you don't think he did."

"I've no reason to," Cellini assured her. "I

want to know if you've any reason to believe it, Mary."

"*No*," she breathed. "He's the very last man—"

"Ryall?" he asked, before she could finish.

"R-Ryall?" she faltered.

"Do you think he killed Lionel?"

"But why should he?" she asked. "He—" She broke off but Cellini did not prompt her. He heard a chink of sound at the door and guessed that it was the nurse with the warm milk, but there was no tap and the door did not open. "Why *should* he?" Mary repeated. "He's always said Joshua wasn't strong enough to be the Patriarch, that he lacked strength where it was most needed, especially in dealing with the outside world, so things were bound to go wrong. Lionel—the way Lionel behaved proved that Ryall was right, didn't it?" She let Cellini take her hands now but he was not sure that she fully trusted him; more likely she wanted to convince him that there was no reason at all to suspect either Joshua Smith or Samuel Ryall. Her fingers were cool and dry.

"I'm sure you're right," he said. "I'm sorry I've worried you, Mary, but I had to find out if there was anything you could tell me to help. Don't worry more than you can. You're quite comfortable here, aren't you?"

"Yes, lovely," she said, withdrawing her gaze.

"Then I should stay here until it's all over," he

encouraged. "Good night, my dear." He turned and stepped quickly to the door, looking at her as he did so.

The door opened.

He kicked against it, sending it flying back, and on the instant there was a gasp, a sound of crockery breaking, another gasp as of pain, and a crash. As Cellini backed into the room the door opened wider, and there was the nurse, empty-handed, the broken mug of milk on the floor, milk all over the place, and a huge damp patch on the nurse's blouse and skirt. A policeman was staring in dismay, and a man from below called curiously: "You all right, Bob?" and came running up the stairs.

"Oh, I *am* sorry," Cellini exclaimed. "And I'd actually heard the chink. I was in such a hurry—" He broke off as the nurse pulled at her soaked blouse as if to prevent its clamminess from touching her skin. She said tersely:

"What a clumsy thing to do."

"I really am sorry—"

"It's no use standing there and saying you're sorry! I'll have to change, and I haven't a thing to get into here!" He had never seen her look as waspish as she did now. "You'll have to stay with her until I'm back."

"I really can't," Cellini interrupted. "I *must* see Carol Smith, it's essential."

"I'll sit in for you, Hilda," the policeman offered. "That's if the young lady doesn't mind. It won't take you long to get a change of clothes, will it?"

"Oh, I suppose not," the nurse said, ungraciously, and went across to the bed, still holding the blouse away from her bosom. "You'll be all right for ten minutes, dear, won't you?"

"Yes, of course," Mary assured her.

"I won't be long." The nurse turned round and almost bumped into Cellini, who hadn't gone after all. "If you do need anything just ring the bell by the side of your bed, Mrs. Tompkins will come at once then." She looked at Cellini more in exasperation than in anger, and said in a more friendly tone: "Well, it *was* a clumsy thing to do, wasn't it?"

"Yes," Cellini admitted humbly. "I'm all fingers and thumbs tonight. I suppose it's because I'm tired. But I *must* see Carol. Can I make some amends by giving you a lift to your home?" he added, torn between courtesy and urgency.

"Oh I only live round the corner," the nurse said.

"Well, if you're sure—" Cellini turned at once with a cursory wave to the girl in the bed, and then hurried past the cordon of policemen and out into the cool street to the car. Dimitry was standing by the side of it, talking to one of the duty policemen. He pulled the passenger door open quickly.

"Everything all right, sir?"

"As far as it can be all right before we know the whole truth," Cellini said, and before getting in he said to the other policeman: "Mary Wilberforce must not be given anything to eat or drink by the nurse, or by anyone, until Mr. Hardy, Mr. Scobie or I say so." He got in as the man promised: "I'll see to it, sir."

"It is of vital importance. Now—Police Constable Bessington's place, please," he said to Dimitry, and dropped down into his seat. A voice sounded over the walkie-talkie radio, and as the other door slammed he asked: "Has any news come over this source of perpetual voices?"

Dimitry shook his head.

"Nothing, sir."

"Humph. Pity." The car moved off quickly and pushed him back against his seat but he did not appear to notice as he stared at the houses on either side. "How far is it from here to Carol—I mean Miss Bessington?"

"A ten-minute drive, sir."

"As much as that!"

"Unless I break every rule in the book, sir!"

"Break them," Cellini said, suddenly imperious. "Get me there just as quickly as you can." He sat very upright as Dimitry put on speed, and in the deserted streets speed did not seem to matter. A policeman appeared here and there but none signalled and no one attempted to slow them down. If Dimitry wondered why there was such a tearing hurry he did not ask, but he cut

every corner he safely could. Soon they were on
the outskirts of the borough away from Merryfield and in the crescent of tall houses, Park
View, where Police Constable Bessington lived.

Dimitry pulled up outside, but had to double
park.

Two policemen converged and they went
through the same routine as before, even to
Cellini being asked for identification. As they
went into the house a church clock nearby struck
three: the *three* clanged on the closing of the
door and the roar somewhere nearby of a car engine. One of the largest policemen Cellini had
ever seen was outside the door of the top-floor
flat.

"Hallo, Adam," this man said. "Good evening,
Doctor."

"Are they asleep, do you know?" asked Cellini.

"They weren't half an hour ago, sir, Bess—
Constable Bessington, I beg your pardon,
brought me out a cuppa. She gave me a key just
in case I wanted to get in, so that I wouldn't have
to ring the bell and wake the patient if she did
drop off." He took the key from his pocket and
inserted it into the keyhole with great care and
precision, making no sound at all. Then he
pushed open the door which squeaked faintly,
but the sound was hardly audible above the soft
tones of music coming from a room, the door of
which was wide open; light came through, subdued and pleasant. The music was immediately

ecognisable to Cellini: Beethoven's Seventh
Symphony in one of its quieter phases. It became
louder as the brass and the wind instruments
joined the strings. "*Now* I can ring the bell, sir,
they're awake. Scare the wits out of them if we
just appeared!" They were a humane lot at
Halling Division, Cellini reflected with one part
of his mind.

The policeman went out and pressed the bell.
Almost as soon as it sounded Bess appeared, tall
and regal-looking in an ankle-length housecoat,
hair drawn to one side carelessly in a way which
accentuated both her sharp features and the
smallness and whiteness of her ears.

"Oh, hallo," she said. "Hallo, Dr. Cellini!" Her
eyes kindled. "I didn't expect to see you at this
hour."

"No, I don't suppose you did," Cellini said,
only half-smiling. "How is Carol?"

"Much better," Bess replied. "In fact I would
say almost herself." She lowered her voice to
add: "I haven't told her what's been happening
at Merryfield, of course. You needn't tell her yet,
need you?"

"I don't think so," Cellini said.

"If only she can have a little time to rest, it will
help her so much."

"I do know," Cellini assured the policewoman,
"and I won't tell her a thing which doesn't seem
to me strictly necessary. But I would like a few
minutes with her alone, Bess."

The tall woman said dubiously: "She's used t
me, now."

"I know," said Cellini. "But I still need a fev
minutes with her alone."

There was a pause; a long pause almost o
conflict. Obviously Bess was not pleased by this
and as obviously Cellini could not insist. H
watched that lean, ascetic face, and studied th
fine brown eyes, expecting her to repeat he
protest, perhaps to call on the huge policeman t
intervene. She was thinking, of course, that h
did not trust her and there was some truth i
that: how could one trust another person abso
lutely, even those about whom one knew a grea
deal? One could take on trust, but that wa
different.

At last, she said, pleading: "you *won't* tell he
about her father, will you?"

"Not unless I absolutely must," said Cellini
"Thank you, Bess. And now, please, I want yo
to humour me still further. Soon, I think we may
have a visitor. If we do I want you to leave al
three of us in the flat together, but keep close t
the front door. You, or that mammoth police
man on duty outside. And stay out, please, unti
you hear me shout. I shall probably shout very
loudly, and when I do please come in quickly
indeed."

Slowly, Bess said: "I suppose you do know
what you are doing."

"I am trying to exorcise a devil," Cellini explained. He moved towards the door in the wake of the policewoman, who stood in the doorway and raised her hand in reassurance to the girl in the room, and said:

"Dr. Cellini has come to have a word with you, Carol."

"Dr. *Who?*"

"Dr. Cellini. You know—"

"Oh, yes," Carol said. "I know who you mean. What on earth can he want with me?"

Cellini went in on the last word.

When he had first glimpsed Carol over Bess's shoulder she had seemed trouble-free, but as he went into the room she reacted much in the way that Mary had, but not as vehemently. Her smile faded, and she looked at him intently, a frown gradually deepening a line between her eyes.

"Carol," he said. "I don't want to ask you any questions about last night. We can forget that, at least for a while. I just want you to cast your mind back to the time before the trouble began at Merryfield."

Her face began to clear.

"That's very easy," she assured him.

"Were you happy?" he asked.

"Oh, wonderfully happy!"

"Did you have boy-friends?"

"Of course, we all did, but—" She broke off, frowned, and said with a curiously flat insistence: "I *was* happy."

"Do you think everybody was?"

"I'm pretty sure they were."

"How could you be sure?" Cellini enquired.

"Well," she said, and as if searching for words, she waved her hands about in front of her. Dark where Mary was fair, with rather narrow features where Mary's were broad, with hazel-coloured eyes, not the clear, clear grey, this girl was the greater beauty, and to some men she would appeal much more than Mary. She had made-up a little, that was no doubt Bess's idea. "Well," she went on, at last, "everybody behaved as if they were happy. They—they laughed a great deal. At the nightly singsongs they—well, everyone let themselves go. There was no furtiveness, no breaking up into little groups." She broke off and then, clenching her fists for emphasis, she cried: "Of course we were happy! Anyone who says we weren't isn't telling the truth!"

"That is exactly what your father told me the first time I went to see him," said Cellini.

"Didn't you believe him?"

"Absolutely. I believed that he believed you were all happy."

"Then why do you ask me?"

"I wondered if a man of his generation could be sure how the young people of yours were feeling," Cellini said.

"Oh, there was no generation gap *then*," Carol said disparagingly. "We lived and worked and played together and it *was* an ideal Community and even though he is my father I'll say that Joshua made it so, he was the heart and soul of it. Even when Ryall challenged him he didn't make a fuss, he simply said it was a matter for the members to decide, that they were far more able to judge whether everyone was happy than he—why, I can remember him laughing and saying gaily: 'What I see going on about me may be wishful thinking!' Everybody laughed, even Ryall. There was a ballot—a secret one so that no member could possibly have any reason not to vote the way they thought. It was absolutely unanimous. Even Ryall said afterwards that it would be ten years before he could hope to be half as good. My father suggested that if he felt the call to lead he should go off and start a small community of his own, but he stayed."

She finished as if uncertainly; as if she were coming out of the past which she had been reliving into the present, and was puzzled by what she said, perhaps as puzzled by the need to defend Joshua and the Community. But she was not distressed; and much of the time her eyes glowed while she was talking. Cellini did not prompt her, while Bess, who was within earshot but out of sight, kept very still.

Slowly, Carol went on: "But it was never really the same after that. Not really the same. It was as if some poison had been sprayed into the air by the conflict, and breathed in by everybody. And—and a lot of us began to think that the

Community was a failure." Her voice trailed away almost to nothing, but the words came out audibly: "I know that I did. I even stopped trusting Joshua. I stopped trusting anybody. And I never did, I just never did understand why."

19

The Visitor

THE WORDS FADED into the silence, yet their ring of fear, of hopelessness, of bewilderment, echoed about the room, and to Emmanuel Cellini there was another ring, a great pleading which, had she put it into words, would have been something like: "Tell me why did it begin? Why, why, why?" Cellini heard a movement behind him and believed that Bess had been so stirred by the tone in the child's voice that she longed to help, could hardly stay where she was, she felt so anxious to give solace. She did not come in, however, and Cellini did not turn to see if she were there; nor to talk to her. He watched Carol and read the hot brilliance of her eyes.

Why, why, why?

And when it seemed that the silence was interminable, and it was like the weight before thunder in the summer air, Cellini said quietly but firmly and in a most matter-of-fact voice: "I think perhaps we can find out."

She gasped: "How?"

"I want you to recall everything you can that happened after the quarrel beween the Patriarch and Samuel Ryall."

"But I've tried. I've racked my brains a thousand times! I can't remember anything that would have started it."

"You don't have to try to prove that what you saw or heard might have started the disruption," rebuked Cellini. "You simply have to remember and tell me."

"How can *you* tell?" demanded Carol, both quieter now, and paler. "How can you possibily tell what could have started this—this awful tragedy?" She answered her own question in the same breath: "You can't! Nobody can!"

"What is the first thing you remember?" asked Cellini, still matter-of-fact.

"You mean—after the trouble between the Patriarch and Samuel Ryall?"

"Yes, of course," Cellini replied with asperity in his tone. "Use your head, Carol. You're not a hysterical child, you've a very good mind. What *is* the first thing you remember? The very first thing which stays in your mind after the confrontation between Samuel Ryall and your father."

She said, huskily: "It was—it was so awful."

"What was awful? Were you attacked?"

"Goodness, no!" she exclaimed, "nothing like that had happened. It was the way Samuel behaved." She stopped again, staring straight in front of her as if picturing some scene, and Cellini had to prompt her again:

"How did he behave?"

"He got *drunk*."

"Ahhh," breathed Cellini. "so Samuel Ryall, the abstemious, the man of such self-control, the challenger to the leadership of the Community, went and drowned his sorrows in drink." He gripped her hand, and said in a laughing voice: "Who told you that was so terrible a thing, Carol? To take too much drink so as to drown a disappointment may not be wise and may be unpleasant and even dangerous for others, but among the human failings it is hardly the worst. Did your father tell you that it was?" When she didn't answer he went on: "Or was it such an offence against the code of the Community that it was regarded by all as a matter of shame?"

Carol answered, in a faraway voice: "It wasn't just that he got drunk."

"Then what else did he do?"

"He—went into Halling and—" Again she broke off and again Cellini had to prompt her but this time all he said was:

"Yes, Carol?"

"He attacked a woman."

"Do you mean he *raped* a woman?"

"No," Carol said, with a little shudder. "No
He—he went into a public house, and the
woman behind the bar wouldn't serve him, and
he struck her."

Cellini did not speak.

"And other men attacked him," went on
Carol, breathlessly. "There was a terrible fight
and he hurt two or three people and did a lot of
damage." Now she spoke very quickly, as if she
wanted to get the story over as quickly as she
could. "The police came and arrested him, and
he was taken to the police station. When—when
the Patriarch heard about it he went to try to get
him released, saying he would make sure he
didn't run away. He had to appear in court next
morning, you see. And—they kept him in the
cells. The Patriarch went to see the Superintendent, Mr. Atkinson, but he wouldn't let Samuel
go, he said he couldn't, it was against the law
So—there was some kind of trial next morning
and—well, I don't understand it, but apparently
he was asked if he wanted to be judged then, and
he said yes, he would like to get it over. They
sent him to prison for three months."

Carol stopped, but she was breathing very
heavily as if still feeling the strain of what had
happened two years ago.

"It was a harsh sentence, I think," said Cellini
gently, "but apparently he attacked the woman
behind the bar without provocation."

"I know he did that," Carol interrupted. "Oh, he deserved to be punished but—but he just didn't understand. He—he wouldn't accept legal help. One of the members is a solicitor, he came to try, but Samuel wouldn't listen to anyone, he said he would take his punishment and be done with it. Three months—" She broke off.

"Carol," asked Cellini, "what distressed you and the others most? The fact that Ryall was sent to prison, or the scandal that it caused? For it must have caused a great deal. Not only do I remember the newspaper headlines, but the Patriarch kept the cuttings, dozens of them. Merryfield was held up to ridicule, wasn't it? From that time onwards there was a sense of shame. Isn't that true?"

"Yes," Carol admitted in a low-pitched voice. "Terrible shame. Until then the people of Halling had respected us, but now they had no respect at all. Gangs of boys would gather at the entrance and jeer whenever our working members went out or came home. There were a lot of little burglaries, youths broke through the hedge—that's why it is so thick and why it's protected now. We even had to ask for police protection."

"Ah," Cellini said. "And did you get it?"

"Oh, yes," she said. "For several weeks there was a policeman on duty at the main entrance, and after that the trouble stopped. But there wasn't the same relationship with the people of

Halling. I suppose that's what went wrong, really. I suppose it *did* begin with the challenge to the Patriarch which started a kind of rot."

"Carol," said Cellini, "did the police come to see the Community?"

"Oh, yes."

"Who came?"

"The Superintendent himself, Mr. Atkinson," answered Carol. "And there was another man with him, a younger man. Oh, they were very good, they did everything they could but—but, well, everything kept on going wrong."

"Did you see Mr. Atkinson there?" asked Cellini.

"Why yes," she said. "We all did. You see, my father showed him over the whole place. It was really the first official visit, and in a way we were very proud and pleased to show the Community off. And—" She paused, but appeared only to be searching for words, and Cellini waited until she went on: "And the Patriarch was so anxious to show the authorities how clean everything was, how well-run. What we were trying to do. Samuel's sentence had started so many stories, we were supposed to be a den of iniquity, every lie people could think of was uttered. Instead of making things better though, the police visit seemed to make things worse."

"Wasn't Mr. Atkinson well impressed?" asked Cellini.

"Well," Carol answered slowly, "at first he seemed to be."

"What changed him?" asked Cellini, softly.

"I don't know. I suppose I don't know if anything did," Carol went on. "He was taken ill."

"*Atkinson* was?"

"Yes," Carol said. "He nearly collapsed. He was with the Patriarch, and a few of us were following. Most of the people stayed in their houses and he visited some of them. He was going to one chalet, and—well, all I know is that he stumbled and nearly fell. He was actually going up to speak to Mary, who had her new baby in her arms."

"Mary Wilberforce?" asked Cellini, and for the first time excitement made his voice quiver.

"Yes," answered Carol. "It was such a shock. He was going towards her and the Patriarch was telling him that this was the newest baby born in the Community, and explaining that after a few months the baby would be looked after partly by the Community and not wholly by the parents. Then he stopped, and if Elizabeth hadn't put her arm round him I'm sure he would have fallen."

There seemed, in that moment, no world except the world in which this girl was living. Even the room seemed part of unreality. So did the sounds outside. A footfall. The closing of the door. An exchange of words in muted voices.

Cellini was aware of all these things yet they seemed the dream, and the story the reality.

The visitor he had expected, indeed had prayed for, had come of course. Bess would do exactly as she was told but would be seething with anxiety and curiosity, and alert every moment for his promised call.

"Tell me *exactly* what happened," he enjoined Carol.

"I—I have!"

"Exactly, Carol, please." He was pleading now. "A small group turned into the garden towards Mary's house, you say. When did the Patriarch tell Mr. Atkinson about the newest baby, and about the baby-care system in the Community?"

"As we were going to the house."

"Was Mary there then?" asked Cellini, tautly. "No. She opened the door with the baby in her arms when the party was half-way between the roadway and the front door. She looked absolutely beautiful," Carol went on, and she herself was lovely, her eyes glowing and her lips moving slowly as if she were savouring what was good of that encounter. "She looked *radiant*. I'd never seen her like it before. She was always pretty, but never like that. I remember I longed to take a photograph, but I hadn't brought my camera. Then—then Mr. Atkinson stumbled, and everything changed. Mary was startled, of course, and the Patriarch ever so alarmed. I've told you if Elizabeth hadn't saved him I'm sure that Mr.

Atkinson would have fallen. Everyone was so upset. It had been such a lovely day, the sun was shining, we felt we were beginning to recover from the shock of what had happened to Samuel Ryall, and this seemed such a happy augury. Then—well, it was just as if it was fated to go wrong."

"I can understand exactly how you felt," said Cellini, "I really can. What happened immediately afterwards, my dear?"

"It was all so confused," Carol answered. "The Patriarch and Elizabeth supported Mr. Atkinson, and the other police officer helped. We wanted to take him to the main house but Mr. Atkinson said he must get home, so the car was brought up to the nearest spot and he was helped into it." Carol raised and dropped her hands. "I really think that was the last time we ever felt really hopeful at the Community. Everything went wrong. Everything. Even the gangs outside the grounds came back, and—well, you know the rest, don't you? That's why the Patriarch sent for you."

Cellini stood up from his chair and remarked quietly: "The trouble began first with Samuel Ryall, then, and became worse after Mr. Atkinson's visit."

"Yes," Carol said. "Yes, that's exactly so." She stood up in turn and moved towards him. Her dressing-gown fell in folds about her feet and she pushed the sleeves back as she looked ea-

gerly into his eyes. "*Can* you help, Dr. Cellini? I
know that my father has great faith in you, that
if anything can be done you will do it." When
Cellini didn't answer, she repeated earnestly:
"*Can* you help?"

From the door, a woman said: "No, he can't.
No one can help. That stinking den of iniquity
has to be destroyed."

Cellini turned round very slowly.

Carol looked past him, in alarm, towards the
door.

The nurse from the police station and the
guest house came in, looking not simply disagreeable but malevolent. Something in the glitter of her eyes would have told most people that
she was not sane.

20

The Devil in Man

NO ONE MOVED behind the nurse.

There was no sign of Police Constable Bessington, no sign of a policeman; only the empty hallway beyond the nurse, who still wore her milk-stained blouse, with dark patches on the skirt and at the breast and who carried, in her right hand, a small automatic pistol; and in her left, what looked like a small bottle of pills.

"Nurse—" began Cellini.

"I'll do the talking," the nurse interrupted, "and there isn't any way you can talk your way out of this. You may be clever as hell, Cellini, but you're not clever enough for that. Move away from the girl."

Cellini said sharply: "Keep behind me, Carol."

"I told you—" began the nurse.

"Nurse!" interrupted Cellini, still sharply, "what possible good do you think this will do?"

"Enough," she said.

"If you think it will save your Mr. Atkinson, you are *quite* wrong," Cellini declared.

The woman caught her breath. Her lips were not only twisted with some inner rage and malevolence but her whole face was distorted. She raised the gun, levelling it at him, and there could be no doubt at all that she needed little encouragement to shoot.

"You're the only one who's guessed," she said thinly. "And I'm going to shut your mouth."

"You will also have to kill Carol," Cellini said.

"That won't be a hardship," the nurse sneered. "The promiscuous little bitch ought to be dead, anyhow, then she can't go round seducing the husbands of other women."

"And once we are gone, her father—"

"He won't live the night out," the nurse said, savagely.

"What on earth does she mean?" gasped Carol.

She was partly behind Cellini, and partly alongside him. He held her arm but if the woman in front of them did shoot there was no way to save the girl. There seemed no way to save himself, either, for reason would not quieten the woman who stood there. She was possessed by hate, strongest of all humankind's emotions, and it was both strengthened and warped by what she must feel for Atkinson; by the love she undoubtedly bore him.

Cellini said quietly: "Stay behind me, Carol."

"*What does she mean?*"

"I mean I went into Merryfield saying I wanted to talk to your father about you and gave him *and* Ryall a dose of morphia strong enough to kill them both," the nurse said, her words running into each other. "I mixed it in some peppermint tablets! And I turned on the broadcasting system to create noises and crackling."

"No!" gasped Carol. "No!" She tried to free herself and to throw herself forward but Cellini, taking a different grip on her wrist, prevented her. She actually kicked him behind one knee, got free and rushed away but stumbled against a big couch and fell into it, so that the woman with the automatic had to try to look two ways at once. "He mustn't die, he mustn't die!" Carol cried, and tried to scramble up.

"Nurse," said Cellini, "both Chief Superintendent Hardy and Scobie know."

"That's a lie!" the nurse cried. "It's a lie!"

Yes, Cellini thought to himself, it was a lie; but it was one which might save his life and Carol's: there was at least a slender chance, and he had only one other.

"It is true," he said sharply.

"If it were true they would have acted by now!" She screeched the words. The glitter in her eyes was maniacal, she spat and spluttered saliva as she cried the words.

"No," he said. "They think they can wait until Atkinson dies."

"Of course he'll die," she said. "He can't live much longer. But they wouldn't wait, they would crucify him for every minute he's got left. Do you think I don't know? They would crucify him. They don't care what happens up in that devil's nest at Merryfield. They'll shut their eyes to farmyard morals, they'll defy the will of God, but they'd crucify Reggie if they ever discovered what he'd done."

"Nurse," Cellini said, "you might still be able to help him."

"No," Carol was saying in a whisper. "No, no, no," and after a pause: "Daddy, oh, Daddy."

"I'll help him by making sure no one knows," the nurse said stridently. "And if it hadn't been for you no one would ever have known."

"Oh, don't be silly," Cellini said testily, and then added in a sharp but not loud aside: "Don't move, Carol, please." He went on to the nurse: "Anyone who saw Mary Wilberforce and Reggie Atkinson together, and realised that the man had been deeply shocked by the encounter, would be curious. And when he began to ask why, the answer would be obvious. There is a marked similarity of eyebrows and forehead. She is his daughter. His marriage failed and the mother and child joined the Community, but he did not realize that until the day he came there and saw Mary with her second child. Isn't that right, Nurse?"

"Yes," the nurse said in a strident voice. "That's exactly right. His wife left him for some soft-tongued Don Juan who said he would show her the perfect life for her and Mary. What Reggie didn't know was that they went to Merryfield. He was over in North London then, he didn't know Merryfield or anything about it. But his wife died in the stinking hole the man took her to, and he never saw her again. He hadn't seen Mary, either, not in ten years, until he saw her holding that bastard brat in her arms. I can tell you this," she went on, swinging round towards Carol. "Your bloody father was boasting that people didn't have to be married in that den of vice, they only had to live together, and it didn't matter about children as the Community would look after them. It's a wonder Reggie didn't die on the spot!"

"Did you know him when he was happily married?" enquired Cellini.

"Of course I knew him, he got me the job as first aid nurse at the station. And I've suffered with him and watched him suffer."

"Until at last, he could stand it no longer," Cellini said, almost musingly. "He knew that Wilberforce was a philanderer, knew that he wasn't even obeying the code of the Community, so last night he followed Wilberforce and Carol—"

"That's where you're wrong!" The nurse sliced across his words. "He knew where Wilberforce always took his whores and he was waiting for them in his car. And when he'd seen him treat her as if she was the only girl he'd ever touched, he got out and choked the life out of the swine. That's what happened, and if ever a man deserved to die it was that seducer of innocent girls and married women. I heard the life rasping out. *I heard it.*"

"So you were there, too," Cellini remarked quietly.

He was aware of Carol, out of the corner of his eyes. She was half-sitting on the floor, half-leaning against the couch, and she appeared appalled by what she heard, she could not keep her gaze off the nurse.

"Of course I was there! I wouldn't let Reggie go out on his own, would I? The excitement might have brought on an attack—of course I was there! I've dedicated my life to Reggie and I'm not going to let you or anyone else crucify him. He's a good man, he—"

Cellini said, in an icy voice: "So after your Reggie had killed Lionel Wilberforce, you tried to kill Carol." That was a statement more than a question.

The nurse drew in her breath sharply:

"Supposing I did. She's nothing but a whore, she deserved to die."

"I wonder who, in your opinion, deserves to live," remarked Cellini still coldly.

"No one in that place of sin! Every man and woman and child there should be wiped out, in the name of the Lord they ought to be destroyed!"

"And you and Reggie, one way and another, were destroying them," Cellini said. "You took advantage of the quarrel between the Patriarch and Ryall, you spread the rumours through Halling about the licentiousness at the Community. You turned the local community against Merryfield, and finally when the time was ripe, you killed Wilberforce, knowing that it would break the Community wide open, that a member, or several members, would surely be suspected. And you and your Reggie were looking forward to it as you'd never looked forward to anything in your life! Reggie would have conducted the investigation and turned it into a hate campaign. He was all set for it, and you were all set to help—and then you found that Chief Superintendent Hardy was already involved. Your hands—Reggie's hands—were tied."

Carol was on one knee, now, supporting herself against the couch. Utterly distraught, her eyes as wild as the nurse's, she seemed to be preparing to leap at the other woman.

"Carol," he pleaded. "Don't try to—"

The nurse swung her gun round towards the girl, rasping: "You'd better not try anything, you slut."

The venom in her voice, the glitter in her eyes, the tension which showed in the back of her right hand, the gunhand, combined to warn Cellini that at last she was going to shoot. And he roared in a mighty voice: "*Carol!*" and at the same time threw himself bodily towards the nurse. Carol slipped in sudden alarm, the nurse swung round, gun now pointing at Cellini, who simply struck her arm aside, a fraction of a second before she fired. The shot cracked. Cellini felt a sharp pain at his left arm. The door crashed open as Carol flung herself upon the nurse who kicked and writhed and screamed in fury, but before she could shoot again the huge policeman had hold of her wrists. The pistol dropped. Bess was paralyzed in a moment of incredulity, then ran towards Carol. Footsteps thundered on the stairs. The big man was bending over the nurse, who lay face downwards on the floor.

Dimitry came running in.

"Bess!" he exclaimed, and then pulled up, staring at the nurse. "Nurse!" His voice croaked. "What—"

He stopped.

It was ten minutes before the nurse was downstairs and on her way to the police station, held on the charge of causing grievous bodily harm.

Ten minutes before the news was relayed to
John Hardy and John Bull. Fifteen minutes before the men on duty at Park View really began
to accept the fact that the nurse was one of the
guilty. Twenty minutes before word came, by
walkie-talkie radio, that a track suit with a cowl
and a gauze face mask had been found at the
nurse's flat. Twenty-five minutes before Police
Constable Bessington glanced at the back of
Cellini's left hand, and said:

"Doctor! You're bleeding."

"Oh, dear," said Cellini, looking down. "I believe I am. I thought my arm felt rather sore."

He was in the bathroom, jacket off and white
shirtsleeve rolled up, the slight wound already
bathed, when Hardy and Bull arrived. All the
policemen except Dimitry vanished; Police Constable Bessington also stayed. With Cellini comfortable and Carol, too, coffee was sent for and
laid on a small table in front of the couch. Cellini
told them what had happened and what the
nurse had said. Once or twice Hardy began to interrupt, but each time he checked himself, once
under a glare from Bull.

At last Cellini finished, his coffee already gone
cold.

"Manny," Hardy said, at last. "You ought to be
shot."

"I was," Cellini retorted, meekly.

"Why on earth did you come here from the
guest house without warning us?"

"I did not dare to warn you in advance," said Dr. Cellini, with dignity. "It would have been done over the police radio, and I suspected that the nurse had a receiver, so she could have known. But I was not greatly worried," Cellini went on. "When she talked about getting a milk drink at that juncture I suspected that she might be trying to poison Mary, probably with morphine in the milk which I so clumsily knocked over. Certainly after what happened to Smith and Ryall I was determined no one should give the child anything which might be poisoned."

"Why should she want to kill Mary?" asked Carol, helplessly. Her legs were tucked beneath her as she sat at one end of the settee; she had seldom looked more pretty although her eyes were huge, the irises big and dark too, because of fatigue.

"Mary would sooner or later have discovered and betrayed the fact that Atkinson was her father," Cellini answered. "The nurse felt an irresistible compulsion to make sure no one would suspect her Reggie, and the moment the relationship was known he was bound to be suspected. Partly for the same reason, Carol, my dear, she tried to kill your father and Ryall. She would also want to kill them so as to strike what she would regard as a blow from which the Community could not recover."

(Hardy had already told them that both men, although still very ill, would not die. The morphine had mixed badly with the peppermints, and some was actually recovered, undissolved, from the stomach of each man.)

"I'm not sure I agree that you couldn't have warned us," Hardy grumbled. "Mary might have died at a second attempt."

"I did warn your policemen, and in any case the nurse was far too anxious to see why I wanted to get to Carol," Cellini explained. "And by the time I had been to Mary she was beginning to feel really frightened."

"And so more dangerous," remarked Bull.

"Deadly," growled Hardy.

"But talkative," Cellini said. "And I did give the highly intelligent Bess here good reason to be on the *qui vive*, didn't I, Bess?" He almost purred.

"I knew you were up to something," Bess said, "but if I'd known about the gun I don't think—" she broke off, looking at Cellini and shaking her head slowly from side to side.

"The only way I could be sure the nurse would talk was by making her feel absolutely confident that she had me at her mercy," observed Cellini. "I really don't know what alternative method you would have adopted, John, but I seriously doubt whether any would have been more effective."

"My way would not have risked your life, or Carol's, or Mary's—" Hardy began.

Perhaps it was the way Bull looked which

stopped him; perhaps it was Bess's expression, or even that of Dimitry, who could not prevent himself from showing the great man from Scotland Yard how much he disagreed. There were a few moments of speculation about how the nurse had managed to poison the two men and why she had made such a set against Elizabeth.

"Perhaps," said Bull, as if he felt left out too long, "because she thought that Elizabeth had recognised her and was telephoning the police."

"I am sure that is as likely an answer as any," Cellini said, politely. "And I doubt if we shall ever know for certain. John, I hesitate to harass you but at least you will admit there was one task I did not attempt to do for you."

Carol asked: "What was that?"

"Good question," Dimitry said, and added smartly: "If I may express an opinion, sir."

The others ignored him. Bess closed her eyes as if she had suddenly become tired, and Bull nodded slowly. The room was very quiet for a long time, and when Hardy rose from his chair the creaking seemed unnaturally loud. But his: "Yes, I must go and see Atkinson," came quietly. "Will you come with me, John? There should be two, and I don't want a local man to be involved."

"Yes," Bull echoed, and stood up.

They found Atkinson in bed; dead.
He had died from diabetic coma, and it was

apparent that he had not given himself the essential injections of insulin. More: there were the dregs of whisky in a bottle in his living room, evidence that he had deliberately induced such a condition. When in death and so repose, there was much more likeness between him and his daughter, Mary.

It was nearly seven o'clock that morning, when Dr. Cellini at last reached home to find his wife Felisa at first prepared to scold him, but soon, simply to soothe and listen until he fell asleep.

When all the details were known and an official report made and issued to the Press, there was a resurgence of publicity about the Merryfield Community, and on the day that this was published Cellini went to Halling. There, newly promoted Superintendent Scobie fêted him, and he was welcomed warmly by all the police. Driving his old but very bright and shiny bull-nose Morris, he went to Merryfield itself. No one was at the entrance. When he reached the main clearing he found newspapermen mixing with the members, and an air of such lightheartedness as he had never seen there before. First Carol, then Mary, soon Elizabeth, came hurrying to meet him, and on their faces was the kind of happiness which he believed was the birthright of all human beings.

"And what has caused this miracle?" asked Cellini.

"Those two," answered Elizabeth, and she turned and pointed to the two members coming out of the main house. Joshua Smith was on the right and Samuel Ryall on the left. They came eagerly, waving to him, but before they drew up, Elizabeth said:

"They are working together, that is all."

"And nothing now divides them," Carol said.

The two leaders came up, shook hands warmly, and without demur posed for photographs with Emmanuel Cellini, who stood happily between them.

"Oh, we have made and are still making mistakes," said Joshua Smith. "We now know, for instance, that we haven't reached the stage of evolution when marriage can be ignored, so now all our couples have been joined together in a civil ceremony at the Halling registry office. It has set a seal of public approval on us, Dr. Cellini."

"I'm not sure that Dr. Cellini's visit hasn't set a greater seal of approval," Ryall said, and sun glistened on his fine teeth and on his unruly red hair. "We also elect two leaders annually, and if either of us misbehaves he can be thrown out inside a year! We've had the relay system taken away and just have one loudspeaker system which can be heard in the houses but is also broadcast outside. Not that we intend to use it very often."

"Dr. Cellini," Joshua said, "we are going to have a double wedding ceremony here in two weeks' time. Elizabeth and I, and Mary—" he smiled at Cellini's startled expression and went on: "and Samuel here. Do you think your friend Chief Superintendent Hardy could come? We have already sounded out Mr. Scobie, who says that nothing will keep him away. And Detective Sergeants Bessington and Dimitry will be here, too. If you could bring your friend, I—" Joshua broke off as if in genuine horror and held both hands out to Cellini in a strangely reminiscent gesture. "But what is the matter with me? I have not yet asked if you can come!"

"Nothing, absolutely nothing, would keep me away, either," declared Emmanuel Cellini.